I0720879

by Matt "Matman" Herring
originalmatman.weebly.com

Cover Illustration and Aquatic Ape drawings by Emily Drouin
emilyatplay.com

edited by Vincent Ferrante for Monarch Books
monarchcomics.com

design and production by Blake
blakemakesart.com

bulletin board montages by Matt

Dedication (and _Thank You_)

Although this book is an obvious love letter to my childhood, this work is dedicated with so much love to my family; Amy, Beky, Samantha, Sagwa, Wolfgang, Troy, and Nick. Although I look back at my past with such fondness, it is my present that I truly love. Lake life, eh?

Thank you to Meredith, Mark, Sarah, and Chris who have seen (and lived) it all, too. What a crazy ride!

Thank you as always to Vincent Ferrante (and Lisa & Igor) for always being there, to correct a misspelled word (or ten thousand) and be such a wonderful support for this, and everything else I do.

Thank you to everyone who has been a part of my life; past, present, and future. You are the reason I am the way I am...so you are all to blame, some more than others! Maybe you are a part of this story as well...

Thank you to Emily Drouin who did such an amazing job from concept to finished designs. Her talent and passion for this project made it that much better and made me finish even quicker.

Thank you to Blake for (once again) making my books look so much better than I could have hoped.

Thank you to Stan Sakai and your wonderful creation, Usagi Yojimbo. You taught me what a good story reads, feels, and looks like. I'm such a fan I got a Usagi tattoo. THAT is dedication, right?

Thank you to Wesley Stace and his alter ego, John Wesley Harding! For over 30 years your music has had such an impact on my life, making me see things in a different light.

Thank you to Michael Sweet, Robert Sweet, Oz Fox, Perry Richardson, and the entire Stryper family! Thank you for letting me be a part of the 'Yellow And Black' story, that doesn't seem to have an ending...and that is a good thing.

Thank you to Ray West who helped to reinforce that being creative has many outlets and avenues. Also, Ray's Spread Eagle bandmates, Rob DeLuca, Rik DeLuca and Jommy Puledda...you dudes are the best.

Thank you to the wonderful little town of Broad Brook, CT, or, the 'crown jewel' of East Windsor, CT. Interesting that in 1987 when I left town, I couldn't wait to get far away, I thought forever. Now, I look for any chance I can to come back home and yes, I'm lookin' at you, Broad Brook Opera House!!!

Thank you to Doug, Emmy Jo, Freddie, Charlie, and Henrietta, for teaching, entertaining, and always giving me/us a safe place to grow. Every generation needs a New Zoo Revue to cultivate creativity, thank you all so much.

A HUGE thank you and much love to Alice Loves Alien, Amanda Meli, Livesay, and Scott Fish who believed so much in this, they gave me their music, the most personal and precious of gifts.

A special thank you to all of you who support my podcasts and writing projects.

Table of Contents*

*A few additional notes *(at no extra charge)* before we begin! Yes, the chapter titles are named after Barry Manilow songs, and there is nothing wrong with that...now! I will admit here, I was then and still am a huge 'Fanilow' but never was able to admit this until the late 1980s. Some of the greatest songs ever recorded!

As awesome as the time period this book takes place in was, everything smelled like cigarette smoke because people could smoke anywhere. Restaurants offered non-smoking sections, but they were next to the smoking sections, and stunk. Remember that? No offense to smokers....

There is reference in this story to Blue Law. Growing up in Massachusetts, all stores were closed on Sunday and no commerce could take place, at all. Interesting though, you could look at and test-drive a car, but you couldn't buy it until the next day, Monday.

Another negative about the era was the gas shortages and the Energy Crisis in the late 70s. Here, you could only purchase gas if your car's license plate ended with an odd or even number, called Odd/Even Rationing. For more information, read then-President Jimmy Carter's "Crisis of Confidence" speech.

When this story takes place, The Vietnam War had ended just a few years prior. Unfortunately, the brave souls who served and returned were NOT treated like their World War II and Korean War brothers, but a distinct memory growing up, among my father's friends. A huge blight that thankfully was rectified, although not until years later.

**The intellectual properties presented in this book, in words or in pictures, are the property of their respective owners, and neither the author or publisher make any claim of ownership regarding these properties.

***Photographs of the author, his friends, family, and acquaintances are part of the author's private collection, and he has the right or permission to publish them in this book. After all, if there isn't a picture, it never happened.

Thought lost (or hidden) for over 40 years, these amazing sketches were created from eyewitness accounts following the first attack at the Broad Brook Carnival in 1978. Finally unclassified, they appear here for the first time.

INTRODUCTION
"Somewhere Down The Road..."

Amongst all of my writing projects, podcast exploits, and general shenanigans, one of my favorite things that I have created is my all-ages book, *MONKEY SEE... SEA MONKEY!* As a child, my imagination and desire for adventure was insatiable; not an escape from something horrible, just an escape to fun. I had the greatest childhood that, yes, had its issues and struggles, but I was the type of person who could always be able to look for the fun, grab a hold of any sunshine, and make the most of every moment. This is something I hope I have been able to pass on to my daughters and anyone I have come into contact with during my life. The book you are about to read, or read to someone, is an open love letter to my youth and a bygone era, a time that made me the adult I am today. It also made me want to write something that took place in that certain point in my life when life was so much simpler.

In 1977, my life had a massive upheaval, moving from the small farming town of Hampden, MA, to the equally small tobacco town of Broad Brook, CT. A move like this, especially going into 4th Grade, was pretty traumatic, despite the differences between the towns and the people weren't that much. I would be leaving my many friends, my sports teams (go Hampden Giants!), and a life I was very comfortable in to move to a school system I would find out I was behind in (math) and would struggle to this day. The previous year, I worked very hard at getting rid (or at least controlling) a stutter that at the time made me the quiet kid; yes, shocking, I know. One of the catalysts for the change was the Green Meadows 3rd Grade production of "The Elf and The Wishing Well" (I was the Elf) that gave me the love of entertaining and being in the spotlight. Learning lines helped me understand that my brain and mouth moved at different speeds. If I could control one, I would be able to work with the other, and it worked. Sadly, I had to start all over again and for this shy, skinny kid with bad teeth, that wasn't cool at all. I was just becoming my own person and began to understand who I was when my parents hit the start-over button. What saved my young life (I know a bit dramatic, but pretty accurate) was STAR WARS! Because the lines were so long to view it in the theatre, I was not going to see it anytime soon, but I had the comic books and a STAR WARS t-shirt. Wearing it on my first day at Broad Brook Elementary (Class of 1978), a fellow student, Jeff Lloyd, came right up to me and asked, "Do you like STAR WARS?" Saying yes, I was brought to a small group of boys talking about the film and this incredible new world that had opened us to all of us thanks to George Lucas. It would be a month later that I finally got to see it on the big screen and from that initial blast of music and opening scene, it was all over! Star Wars figures, Star Wars cards, Star Wars *anything* and everything!

At this particular time in my life, I was devoted to STAR WARS, comic books, music, hockey, and baseball... so yes, nothing has changed for me. My summers living in a building complex involved waking up early, watching TV while eating

QUISP, King Vitamin, or Captain Crunch, then going out to the community pool and swimming until noon, when my skin and eyes were dried out from the chlorine. After that, I would go home for lunch, walk to Pigeon's Pharmacy or Dairy Mart for comic books, cards, and/or magazines. After the trip, it would be baseball or a game of war in the woods until it got so dark, we couldn't see anything including where we were walking. After a hot bath (and maybe a night swim) it would be the routine of reading comic books and watching TV until bedtime. Following some Star Wars, hockey, music, and baseball dreams, it was wake up and repeat because this is how we lived back then, with slight variations from day to day.

What I loved about this magical time in life is how the 24-hour day seemed to last much longer than the allotted time presented. It also seemed that the New England summer seemed to go on beyond the June-July-August pages on the calendar, it went on so much longer. This is not saying that my life growing up was all Disney and cotton candy, because it wasn't. I just made it that way. Moving a lot (3 times in 1st grade), some family issues, financial struggles, and very challenging interpersonal dynamics (that, sadly, still exist today) could have destroyed me if I just gave into them but I chose a different path. It wasn't denial because I acknowledged they were there, but dealt with the issues when they happened, and decided this wouldn't be what defined me. I would take a lot of the pain and concerns I had and focus on the important things in life...STAR WARS, comic books, music, hockey, and baseball! If only I had applied that drive and devotion to my schoolwork, I would have been voted Most Likely to Succeed in the Class of 1986, like Phil Wielhouwer. Instead, I was voted Class Clown and Most Talkative, two awards that interestingly still serve me well to this day. By the way, Phil went on to serve our country with honor as a fighter pilot and retired a Colonel with honors. Thank you for your sacrifice and service to our country, Phil and family.

What you are about to read is a fantasy that I always had, and possibly one you had, too. Like Luke Skywalker looking at the setting sons of Tatooine (of course with the music swelling around him), I wanted to grow from my small humble place in life and go on to do great, world-changing things. I wanted to be the hero when bad things happened and transform myself into the leader that would not only inspire but show true grace under pressure. The original story that the book you're holding became came out in 2015 and was born from some interesting conversations I was having while doing the comic book/book tour for my 3rd book, THE UNOFFICIAL DOCTOR WHO COMPANION. I don't know exactly when my idea of Sea Monkeys taking over the world formulated, but as Keith Gleason, Amy Kukta Gleason, and I were traveling from Rhode Island Comic Con (where we were exhibiting in late 2014), the basic ideas began to germinate. The story started as a WAR OF THE WORLDS tale, briefly moving into THEY LIVE with a brief stop at LORD OF THE FLIES. The story featured these smiling, cute, creepy, and pink humanoid things pictured in those classic comic book ads. As I kept putting this idea aside to work on other writing projects, this story just kept growing and growing... like a heaping bowl of brine shrimp. Following a weekend at the Northeast Comic Con (thank you Gary Sohmers) and more conversations with Keith and Amy, plus idea bouncing with George O'Connor, Griffin Ess, Chris & Alan Hebert, and some psychic lady, I had no choice but to put this idea down on paper, because this story needs to be told! Well, it doesn't really need to be told, but I want to tell it...and it *really* wasn't put to paper, because we are part of the Microsoft Word generation.

Speaking of WAR OF THE WORLDS, a big part of this story came from listening to the 1979 album, JEFF WAYNE'S MUSICAL VERSION OF WAR OF THE WORLDS. As a kid this audio drama (on two LPs) purchased at Caldors, blew my mind! When I rediscovered it in 2015, the music and acting really gave me a focus of what I wanted to do... tell a story with excitement, unfavorable odds, and invading creatures. I was also inspired by PLANET OF THE APES and THE WARRIORS, especially that hopelessness of an enemy that just comes and comes...and never stops!

I was so fortunate to be a child of the '70s and a teenager in the '80s. I feel I had the absolute best (and worst) of both worlds, and it wasn't always fun and games, but here I'm focusing on the games. I love being able to look at the music of the era and finding magic in all of it, even if I didn't consider it my jam. I wish I had the courage to admit at the time that I loved Barry Manilow, the Bee Gees, and disco music. In fact, I hid my Barry Manilow albums under my bed so no one would see them. And I only publicly admitted my love of the Bee Gees in the late 1980s when Alice Cooper said they were one of his favorite songwriters and performers. And movies? M*A*S*H*, JAWS, LOGAN'S RUN, SLAPSHOT, ANIMAL HOUSE, CLOSE ENCOUNTERS OF THE THIRD KIND, SUPERMAN, APOCALYPSE NOW, THE WARRIORS, and of course STAR WARS...movies that made me feel so many things and inspired me, this story...my entire life. We also only had four TV channels, smoking areas in restaurants, a gas shortage, and one flavor of Gatorade but somehow, we all survived. We had to.

Using the idea of an alien invasion but with Sea Monkeys just sounded like so much fun and so full of visual contrast. Unlike true-life monsters like Nazis (who do make an appearance in the story) or the creepy octopi-inspired Martian invaders from WAR OF THE WORLDS, Sea Monkeys are cute and seem incapable of death and destruction…or so we thought. As I officially decided to look through the old manuscript and give it a fresh coat of paint, my publisher, Monarch Books, wanted this on their 2023 release schedule. So here we go. What year is it? Did I meet the schedule?

As you can imagine, with a real publisher, a serious change had to occur...we couldn't use the name Sea Monkeys because we don't own the rights and we aren't quite sure who does. The previous book was self-published, and everything was done by me. Now I have the power of an editor (Vincent Ferrante) and a real graphics department (Blake), the team that helped make *BLACK SABBATH – THE VINYL TESTAMENT* look so incredible. Since Monarch Comics (and Books) are available everywhere like Amazon, Barnes & Noble, Wal-Mart and select comic book stores, I thought it would be smart and right to change the name up and redesign the characters but maintain the magic of brine shrimp in a bowl that grow big and try to take over the planet! As you saw by the amazing cover by Emily Drouin, the new look creatures are just beautiful, based on a creepy real thing called an Axolotl. If you missed the cover, close the book and look again. I'll still be here waiting.

What I hope *MONKEY SEE... 'SEE' MONKEY* does for, you, young reader, is to entertain you and create a chuckle with a story that comes from a much slower, bygone era; a time without cell phones and the only computers being a calculator or the Little Professor math-teaching game. For the adult reader, I hope this fills your heart with so much nostalgia that you can taste the Mello Yello, Lipton Giggle Noodle Soup, and Zarex. Growing up in the 70s and 80s was a magical time that we can't ever let go of. I think back to the innocence we all had as kids, a time when I used to believe astronauts went to the moon everyday (because my parents went to their jobs everyday) or the stars of a TV show sang the theme songs, it was just fun times.

World War Two gave us the Greatest Generation, so that makes us part of the... umm....other Greatest Generation!

Thank you everyone who had a starring role in this book and in my most awesome life!

- Matt "Matman" Herring

STAR WARS AT CHILD WORLD

MAY THE FORCE GUIDE YOU TO OUR SPECTACULAR SPACE AGE TOYS!

Kenner STAR WARS FIGURES

1 87 Ea.

Choose from Luke Skywalker, Princess Leia Organa, C-3PO, R2D2, Ben (Obi-Wan) Kenobi, Darth Vader, Chewbacca, Han Solo and Stormtrooper. In authentic costume.

Kenner Star Wars Light Saber **3 99**

Safe, soft vinyl blade. Easy to inflate. Lights up at the touch of a button.

Kenner Star Wars X-WING FIGHTER **9 99**

A reproduction of the X-Wing fighter used to destroy Death Star.

Kenner Star Wars LANDSPEEDER **4 99**

A replica of Luke Skywalker's vehicle. Figure not included.

Parker Brothers CLOSE ENCOUNTERS OF THE THIRD KIND **4 97**

First the movie, now the game! For the whole family. Our Reg. 6.99

CHAPTER ONE
"Could It Be Magic?"

Like many of the great battlefields in American history that took place on American soil, like Gettysburg or Bunker Hill (actually fought on Breed's Hill), you don't see the destruction, loss of life and despair anymore. In many cases they may just look like an average field or hill that has grown wild with brush or the home of impromptu kickball games. Today, when I gaze upon the battlefields that, in 1979, changed the course of the entire world, not just the small town of Broad Brook, CT, I'm saddened and shocked that they have already been forgotten as part of this pivotal moment in our history. If this story happened now, not 40 years ago, it would be on YouTube, all over Facebook Live, and coverage on CNN would be nauseating. But there is a serious denial that this ever happened and even some of the players don't or choose *not* to remember. A few years ago, I was at a concert with Jon Martell, Last In Line & Dokken at the MGM in Springfield, MA. Jon was injured in the Battle of Broad Brook (the story you are about to read includes his injury), and he said he didn't remember any of it. Did he choose to forget?

"Dude, I don't remember what happened on my way to this concert," Jon told me, "let alone something that happened a million years ago when we were in 5th Grade." I think he is STILL in denial.

This happens with all the adults today who were just kids in this story. What you are about to read is true…every single word of it. I know at times these ramblings may be hard to believe and even impossible to understand, but this is my story and could have sadly been the last will and testament of the entire human race… cue dramatic music.

As Americans found themselves midway through the 1970s, we became a nation of jaded and paranoid people, just looking for something we could put our faith in. We were still feeling the pain and embarrassment of the lightning rod known as the Vietnam War, a conflict that polarized our nation and made us quite vulnerable. Politically we were trying to forget the shame of disgraced President Richard Nixon and Watergate and stand behind our new President, Jimmy Carter. From the outside, President Carter seemed to be a pretty nice guy with a daughter close to my age, but the former peanut farmer appeared to be in way over his head in the world of politics and foreign intrigue.

Across the oceans we had the ever-growing paranoia of the Soviet Union and their "evil" Communist ways, waiting to bring an end to all the things we loved and held dear. Every night I would go to bed terrified that the dark skies would rain Russian R-36 missiles on my house and every day at noon and 5 PM I would hear the fire siren go off in town and break into a cold sweat because I thought THIS was the well-timed end! As a nation, we had our eyes to the skies with children watching and waiting for the space station, Sky Lab, to crash into their houses.

Christians were waiting for Jesus to return, and others were wondering if the stars they were seeing in the nighttime sky were satellites; some protecting us, others spying us…but many looking to destroy us and our way of life!

It became quite a shock when America's possible downfall and our world's inevitable destruction wouldn't come at the hands of Russian tanks, Chinese soldiers or even this Ayatollah guy from a small country I never even heard of… but from an army of creatures so deceitful, so loathsome and yet so stinkin' cute, but that was the subtle charm. This 'army' would be born in the unsuspecting breeding ground of children's room, schools, and college dorms and sadly, we paid for it with our own hard-earned money… $1.25 plus .50 cents shipping and processing. Little did we know, WE would be the ones being processed!

Our journey and our end began when millions of kids saw an ad in a back of a comic book that promised them "a bowlful of happiness – instant pets," and what child wouldn't want that? Aquatic Apes would be brought into millions of homes the world over and as they grew in their aquatic homes, we waited…and waited… and waited.

In the small, peaceful town of Broad Brook, Connecticut, it seemed that all my friends had Aquatic Apes and were all enjoying the "fun for the whole family" promised in the adverts. That is, everyone had them but me. Years before, my sister (three years my senior), Meredith, ordered these "delightful pets" and, as they got a little older and a little bit bigger, our mom got panicky and dumped them down the toilet, no questions asked, no quarter given.

"I don't want those blueish, crowned-headed things living in my home," she justified as she destroyed an entire colony with just one flush. "I don't want them to take over my home and kill my family while we sleep."

My sister cried her eyes out and my father got a little upset, not because of the death of the Aquatic Apes, but because the flushing incident ruined his enjoyment of the Tuesday night ABC comedy lineup featuring HAPPY DAYS, LAVERNE & SHIRLEY, and THREE'S COMPANY. Maybe my mother was onto something? Somehow, maybe she knew there was something more sinister at play. She knew, as we all did, that what was being sold as harmless brine shrimp weren't harmless at all, and, if left to grow, who knows what could have transpired? She may not have known exactly what was going to happen, but her flushing the neon blue demons made me understand a little more about when they say momma knows best because in this instance, she did!

I don't remember the exact day that everything changed, but I do remember being your typical happy-go-lucky young man enjoying life, liberty, and pursuit of happiness. Back then, I was a fairly tall and very skinny kid with braces (covering some pretty bad teeth) and sporting a haircut like Davy Jones of the Monkees, a decade after The Monkees, so it was now comparable to singer/actor Shawn Cassidy. During this particular summer day, I was with a bunch of friends at the community swimming pool just doing what kids do…nothing but enjoying no school and no rules. A few summers back, I had moved to a large building complex called Mill Pond Village and this summer I was finally beginning to feel comfortable with my new friends, my new school, and my new state. Our days were very simple. We would get to the pool about 9 AM and swim until our lungs hurt. After hours of playing Marco Polo, ladder tag, and THE MAN FROM ATLANTIS we would lay on the cool cement, cooking in the sun without suntan lotion, because real men didn't smell like coconuts. We would have our radios blasting out the hits of the day. That day's selection featured, among others, David Naughton's disco hit, *Makin' It*, and *Stumblin' In* by Suzi Quatro and Chris Norman. Timeless music to go along with timeless fun.

Like clockwork at 12:30 Monday through Friday we would watch the mail delivery arrive, all drooling at the packages being carried into the package room, wondering if any were ours. Here we would watch an assortment of boxes of all shapes, colors, and sizes being brought in, waiting for their owners to come and claim them. The crown jewel of all package deliveries, the one we all coveted, was the Columbia Record and Tape Club package. This one contained your 7 records, cassettes, or 8-track cartridges for just a single buck. Sure, we all forged our parent's signatures and had no intention of buying 8 more at regular club prices over the next few years, but just like that, in one box, we had an instant music collection! Life was good for all of us, especially if you got a package. Seeing the mail guy leave, I wrapped a towel around me, and, against the office rules, went barefoot into the mail room. I walked straight in and unlocked the small metal door that said 5-F on the front. Crammed inside the little 5 by 5-inch box were a few bills for my mom, a copy of FUR FISH AND GAME for my dad, my crumpled brown paper-wrapped copy of INVADERS # 31 (mailed flat, my eye!) and the latest issue of the family newspaper, GRIT! But something was missing… "Still no Boba Fett figure?" I mumbled, disappointed yet again, slamming the little metal door shut. "How long is six to eight weeks?"

GRIT was the true voice of the people as far as I was concerned. The adults had ROLLING STONE and old people had LIFE, but we had GRIT! To me it was if Paul Harvey had his own newspaper because GRIT contained some real news stories from all over the country, fiction tales, and comic strips, one-stop shopping at its finest. As I brought the pile of mail to the pool and dumped it on my towel, I slipped my burning feet into the over-chlorinated, cloudy blue water and flipped open my paper. There was something cool and so adult about reading a newspaper. I turned to the fiction section and began to read something that not only grabbed my attention but made my little heart race with excitement. The story was called "Instant Soldiers, Just Add Water" and was a fascinating tale about a German scientist who in the 1940s was working for the Nazis using his skills to further the German war effort in a scientific and very creepy way. This man's objective was to create a race of super soldiers, ones that could be grown in any climate and be able to adapt to any situation they found themselves in. This would help replenish the "real" soldiers that were dying all over Europe to keep the war going for Hitler and his goons. His goal was to drop the instant soldiers onto the snows of Russia and then, poof, soldiers would grow from the snow and continue to fight.

"Fascinating," I thought as I read more!

The writer continued this captivating story by telling us about how, after the war, when escaped Nazis were being hunted down, this scientist, who hid his Jewish bloodline from his bosses, escaped capture in Europe. He then somehow snuck into the United States and settled somewhere in Tennessee. This diabolical man then began to rewrite his entire history, claiming on all his personal documents that he was born in Memphis. His goal was to somehow use these genetic creatures he created to be soldiers that were never perfected for the Third Reich. His plans included making an even crazier and more hateful *Fourth* Reich. As a bonus, he would make a lot of money selling stuff to kids. Sadly, all this craziness was happening right under our very noses.

At this point in my life, it was all about comic books, STAR WARS, and Beth, the cute girl who sat in front of me last year in 4th grade. She was as dreamy as Princess Leia and Kristy McNichol all rolled into one! Her perfect hair and tartan wardrobe were, well, perfect. But this story was making me forget about all of that and inspired me to put pen to paper and write a letter to GRIT. In those days it was everyone's dream to get a letter published in a comic book, newspaper, or magazine. I was so inspired by the story that the words flowed from my blue Bic Banana pen like those guys who wrote the Constitution, all of them. In my eloquent letter I told the editors how much I loved the story about the Nazi scientist and hoped to see more from this particular writer because in my own well thought-out words, "the story was wicked cool!"

A few weeks later, following the usual swimming and mail room routine, I was excited to get a letter from GRIT featuring an embossed envelope with the word GRIT in dark blue coming straight from their headquarters in Topeka, Kansas! This was no Boba Fett figure or wrinkled-up comic books, and yet my knees began to shake, I got a little lightheaded, and I couldn't breathe. A letter from GRIT?! Should I run home and read it?! Should I bring it to the pool and impress everyone?! After all, this was a real live letter from a national publication, and it deserved its due respect! So, while I stood there in the mail room, I tore into the envelope, shredding it with my own excitement, and carefully pulled out the typed letter.

"Dear Matthew," the letter opened, sending chills down my spine because it was addressed to me! "Thank you for taking the time to write us and let us know how much you enjoyed the story, "Instant Soldiers, Just Add Water." We always love to hear from young readers such as yourself and know that your enthusiasm will ensure GRIT to survive forever." Yup, I was making a difference, but it was the last part of the letter that really freaked me out. "But I must admit to you that when we were putting that particular issue together, that story wasn't a part of it, and we don't know where it came from. When the paper was printed, it was brought to our attention, and we all wondered how this story even got into the issue. I know how his sounds; like a mystery that Encyclopedia Brown or the Hardy Boys should be investigating, but we don't have any clue about the writer of the story or how the story even got printed. We don't even know how to pay him or hire him to write more exciting stories that would be featured in America's Greatest Family Newspaper, GRIT! Sincerely, Hobart Sunsby – Senior Editor and Publisher of GRIT"

WOW! This was a real live letter right from the editor, Mr. Sunsby himself! I bet he is so important he knows what KISS look like without their make-up! That was so cool, but I didn't quite know what to make of what I just read. I needed an adult's help in figuring all this out, so I waited for later that night and some time alone with my dad. How can a story get printed without anyone knowing about it? Later that night, our Spirit of '76 TV trays were in full extension, bowls of food cooling, and SHA NA NA was on the television.

"Do you know they played at Woodstock?" my dad asked me, like he asked me every time we watched the show. "Jimi Hendrix, The Who, Joe Cocker and Sha Na Na!" I wasn't impressed with that factoid then, but now... so *cool*.

I always answered "no" and then got the full details how this doo-wop band played the biggest music event in the history of the planet. But, before he could start taking, I handed him the letter. Over our hearty bowls of Hamburger Helper Wagon Wheels, my dad perused the typed paper carefully, folded it back up, and handed it to me.

"This letter is just a clever trick by a shrewd businessman," he told me, enjoying the spicy pasta, meat, and wagon wheel shapes thanks to Betty Crocker. "They just want you to keep reading GRIT and what better way to keep you interested than to have a mysterious story, a crazy event, and a letter campaign. Is your subscription ending soon?"

Sadly, I shook my head yes, realizing this probably was more of a way to get me to renew my subscription. Fair enough, I thought to myself, feeling a bit deflated and let down. A part of me believed what my dad told me as the facts, but another part of me wanted there to be more to this than just some gimmick; a true real-life adventure... featuring *Nazis!*

I thought this Nazi scientist thing was all over and didn't give it anymore thought until a few days later when *another* letter arrived for me. I began to think something was really up because I just *didn't* get letters from *anyone!* I wasn't a teenager with a pen pal! But there it was, another letter with my name and address on it. But I grew a little cautious because there was no return address on it. We learned last year in school how to properly write a letter and address an envelope, and, so far, this one was a big fat F! Maybe it was a chain letter thing I heard about or maybe some weirdo had my address and was going to try and hurt me via the US Postal System. I wouldn't know until I opened the letter, so I stuck my finger under the flap and let it rip!!! Like Parker Stevenson and Shawn Cassidy, I carefully looked over the letter for poison, bombs, or even clues. Since I didn't see any, I just opened the letter and began to read it. What I read would change my life and the fate of the entire world, all in that order.

... and still no #$%^&@# Boba Fett figure!

"Dear Matt! I saw your letter and want to personally thank you for your excitement about the story I wrote. But I need to tell you that this tale wasn't a work of fiction but something that is true and happening right now! This is reality, and anyone I try to explain this to just laughs at me. To put myself through school I took a job answering phones for the Poison Control Center Hotline right near my college. As a Journalism major, I was hoping to make a little extra cash as well as hear some crazy stories that may help me to write the next great novel, like THE BOYS FROM BRAZIL, JAWS, or RAISE THE TITANIC. Late one night I received a weird call from a frantic mother from New Hampshire. A few minutes earlier this woman's daughter drank a small cup containing Aquatic Apes and was concerned that she was going to die because there were no warnings about them on the packaging. "There was no Mr. Yuk sticker on the cup," she kept telling me, "THERE WAS NO MR. YUK!" She was in a panic and didn't know what to do. She was feeling guilty like she just let this happen and was now responsible for these things now growing in her child's body that were going to rip and claw their way out. I told her to remain calm and have her daughter drink a can of Coke with a Pop Rocks chaser. That should kill any foreign bodies living inside her. And if that didn't reassure her, I told her to just stick her fingers down her throat and make her puke."

I couldn't believe what I was reading! This was fantastic, gross, and amazing…

"I wrote the call down in the logbook that we are required to keep and told Hope, the girl working next to me, about the weird call. She was cute, Canadian, and I was always looking for any reason to talk to her, so this was good. She looked at me funny as she sipped her Fresca straight from the can and told me that she had a similar Aquatic Apes-related call a few weeks ago from a guy in Pueblo, Colorado. A man put an Alka Seltzer tablet into a cup that he thought was regular water, but it contained his son's Aquatic Apes. Later on, with a little investigating, I would discover that many others were getting similar Aquatic Apes calls. And soon we were getting inundated with Aquatic Apes-related problems…I knew something was certainly amiss."

Aquatic Apes? Those things are a total rip and don't even work.

"Something was up, so I decided to do a little snooping around. I discovered that Aquatic Apes were created and packaged in a place in Memphis, Tennessee at the Freeze-Dried Institute, or the FDI for short. They shared a building with Fluoridate America; a company that made fluoride used in toothpastes like Crest and Colgate, and also provided fluoride to communities that were fluoridating their drinking water. So, while I was on a break from college I went down there, took a job as a janitor, and began to snoop around."

The letter went on and on with the writer telling me how he got deep into the operations at the FDI, and in his disguise was able to secure some top-secret documents that were strangely just lying around all over the place, with some of them in the trash. I bet the papers smelled like those sweet-smelling ditto sheets from school. I read on…

"As I was cleaning the office of this German guy who created Aquatic Apes, I was horrified to find out that there was something diabolical going on behind the scenes. I saw a document that was meant to be destroyed explaining how these harmless pets would grow and spread terror first in people's homes and then the unsuspecting towns and communities that were targeted. From what I could gather, these Aquatic Apes would not only destroy everything we hold near and dear but could also bring about the downfall of humanity, even Commies! But how and where was all this going to happen? I'm not exactly sure, but if people are in the know then we can be ready to beat it back when it begins to happen. Please help me in spreading the word and join in the fight against this unimaginable evil!"

The letter was simply signed "Jeff."

Double Wow again! If I didn't take this too seriously, it was probably because my ten-year-old brain couldn't handle it if I thought any of this was actually real. But because I read a lot of war comics and saw a lot of war movies, I would know what to do in the event of invasion. But really, *Aquatic Apes?* How could something we barely could see rise up to do anything other than make a little mess if it spilled on shag carpeting or in a beanbag chair? There…I just figured out how to beat them…tip their container over and then the threat is over. When my mother flushed my sister's instant pets down the toilet, I was never convinced they even existed because I never even saw them floating around their bowl. It always just looked like nothing but a cloudy glass of water, but apparently there was something alive in there…something evil and lurking below the surface.

Later that evening, my brain was all fired up with this crazy chain of events that seemed to be unfolding right in front of me. Apparently, I was at least a little convinced that something was going on despite my cavalier attitude. I decided I wasn't going to say anything about this to anyone in case this was all just a hoax or a joke and give people a reason to make fun of me. After all, I was just beginning to fit in and didn't want to rock the boat in any way. So far, I have been able to hide my asthma from everyone because the combination of asthma, comic books, and sci-fi could be deadly for a kid heading into Middle School. But before I went to sleep that night, I pulled out my MOUSE TRAP game. "Roll the dice and move your mice," I said reciting the TV commercial, removing the pieces, and setting up the board on my bed. Using a few green army men, I drew up, or at least played out, the plan of how I would help save the world using multicolored mice, a plastic bathtub, and some dice. This stupid game never worked anyway like it did on the commercial, but tonight I sure needed it to! I wrote down some detailed notes and drew up a fail-proof battle plan that would ensure the survival of humanity…or at least my survival. Once it was completed, I tucked the papers away into my cool blue Trapper Keeper notebook that I would be using in 6th Grade like a big boy, and placed it safely under my bed next to my Barry Manilow albums. Then, with the entire weight of the world on my bony little shoulders, I just went to sleep.

When I woke up the next morning all the fire and determination that I went to bed with seemed to be all gone. I wasn't caring so much about these Aquatic Apes anymore and got to work on a more pressing matter, finding my swimming trunks and a dry towel. The rule is you are not supposed to swim on an empty stomach, so I downed a couple of heaping bowls of QUISP cereal and got ready to go. Grabbing a bottle of Mello Yello, the fastest soft drink ever, I took the tour of the building complex, collecting friends for yet another lazy day of swimming and burning our exposed feet on the hot pavement, because real men didn't wear Flip Flops! We were kids, we had rules, and that is what we did. So, gathering up Kevin, Cindy, Bobby, and Amy, we made our way to the shimmering siren song called the Mill Pond Pool.

Getting Kevin sometimes was a little difficult, and I had to be a bit clever. Before I would knock on the door, I would press my ear to it and listen if his brother Mark was up and around. If he was, I would just leave. Any time I was alone with Mark it would end up with him beating me up in what we called the orange room because the room was painted orange. We were clever. And Mark was a B-I-G boy. He would lift me over his head, push my face into the ceiling, and practice his best Gorilla Monsoon or Chief Jay Strongbow moves while listening to the classic album, TED NUGENT. "Stranglehold," "Stormtroopin," "Dog Eat Dog," "Snakeskin Cowboy"…all great songs I can't listen to it anymore without shaking. I was beat up in full view of two Aerosmith posters that made me stay away from that band for years, due to trauma. I didn't watch wrestling yet, so I didn't know what to do to get out of these holds. Now I was more careful.

Waiting for us at the pool would always be Brenda and Kerry who always got there a few hours before everyone else. Without a single care in the world we would swim, lie out in the sun, and dry off, then repeat the process about fifty more times throughout the course of the afternoon. As we splashed around playing ladder tag we were unaware that just a few miles up the street, the possible end of days was entering its first moments.

204 REVOLUTIONARY WAR SOLDIERS
Only $1.98

2 COMPLETE ARMIES
EVERY PIECE OF PURE MOLDED PLASTIC—EACH ON ITS OWN BASE
UP TO 4" LONG! TWO COMPLETE ARMIES—THE BRITISH RED-
COATS AND THE AMERICAN BLUECOATS! RELIVE AGAIN THE
FAMOUS BATTLES OF THE AMERICAN REVOLUTION! FORM
YOUR OWN BATTLE LINES! HOURS OF FUN
FOR THE WHOLE FAMILY!

HERE'S WHAT
YOU GET:
36 Dragoons (Cavalrymen)
12 Shooting Infantrymen
12 Marching Infantrymen
12 Crouching Infantrymen
12 Filers
12 Charging Infantrymen
12 Sharpshooters
12 Field Cannon
12 Cannon Loaders
12 Drummers
12 Minute Men
24 Mohawk Indians
12 Officers
12 Hessian Troops

RUSH COUPON TODAY

Revolutionary War Soldiers
Dept. BW4K . Carle Place, Long Island, N. Y.

Gentlemen:
Here's my $1.98. Rush 204 Revolutionary War
Soldiers to me. If not satisfied I may return
merchandise for full refund!

Name
Address
City ____ Zone ____ State ____
Canadian orders: Send international money order for $3.50.

207 STAMPS 25¢
plus 88 FLAGS OF THE WORLD
plus ALL 14 CONFEDERATE
STATES FACSIMILES IN COLOR
yours for only

88 Flags of
all Nations

TOGO

What a tremendous bargain this is! You get every single one of
the stamps pictured here – plus hundreds of other fascinating
issues from all over the world! 207 Stamps in all – a wonderful
start – a big boost for your collection!

But that's only the beginning! You also receive 88 different
"Flags of the World" – in glowing full color – to dress up the
pages in your album. Then you get all 14 Confederate Facsimiles.

Yes – you get ALL of these items – plus the interesting and
informative "Midget Encyclopedia of Stamp Collecting" – ALL
for only 25¢! We'll also include – on approval – a big selection
of other unusual stamps and sets. You may purchase any of
these Approvals at Zenith's low prices – and return the remainder within 10 days. But whether or not you buy any of the
approvals – the 207 Stamps, 88 Flags and 14 Confederate Facsimiles are yours to keep for only a quarter! Mail coupon NOW

SEND 25¢ WITH COUPON TODAY!

ZENITH COMPANY, Dept. NG-46
81 Willoughby St., Brooklyn 1, N. Y.

Rush me my 207 Stamps, 88 Flags, 14 Confederate
Facsimiles and Midget Encyclopedia of Stamp Collecting. I enclose 25¢ in full payment.

I will also receive – on approval – a selection
of other unusual stamps and sets. I may buy as
many or as few (or none at all) of these Approvals
at your low prices . . . and agree to return the
remainder within 10 days.

Name
Address
City ____ Zone ____ State ____
(please print)

FREE: Midget Encyclopedia of Stamp Collecting
ZENITH CO. 81 Willoughby St. Brooklyn 1 N. Y.

hair
teeth
STAR WARS
FREE
16 Trading Cards
Best of Luck to the Class of "79"
From PIGEON'S PHARMACY
Main St — Bound Brook
15¢ Marathon 15¢
Good for one Marathon Bar
or 15¢ off on a Marathon six-pack
STORE COUPON
Check
$1.98
STAR WARS
LUKE SKYWALKER
OPERA HOUSE
BINGO
5 16 44 47 62
13 20 33 49 64
9 23 52 63
15 25 36 60 66
11 22 41 50 67
WATER TOWER

CHAPTER TWO
"Weekend In New England"

One of the biggest events of the summer in the life of anyone from Broad Brook, especially a kid, is the legendary Broad Brook Carnival. For three fun-filled days and two crazy nights in July, you are able to ride the terrifying rides, like the Ferris Wheel, that you thought was actually going to break when there were more than two people on it. THAT alone made it terrifying. You could buy fried dough with your choice of sugar or pasta sauce that may or may not react with whatever you ate prior and take a chance at Lion's Club Bingo with cash prizes. If you played your cards right and found the secret locations (usually by accident), you could sneak over and watch the big kids drink, smoke, and even make out. Actually, the secret location wasn't a very big secret. It was at the far end of the field behind the row of blue and green Port-a-Johns. Or you could just follow the drunk teenagers trying to act sober, or the sober ones trying to act drunk. This event became the highlight of our summer fun, especially on Saturday night when the parade came rolling down Main Street with all the bells and whistles. In the days leading up to this year's event, something seemed a bit off and a little bit weird...so much you could feel it in the air. You didn't need to be a cow circling in the field to know that rain was coming… and cows were an East Windsor institution, and cow tipping a sport you could take in school. My sister and her friends lettered in it.

With a few bucks in my pocket, or in my shoe, because my swim trunks had no pockets, I took an early evening stroll to Pigeon's Pharmacy, probably my favorite place in the entire world! When I first moved to Broad Brook, Pigeon's Pharmacy became the place I would go to and forget about my sadness for leaving my old friends and everything I knew. Here I could get comic books, magazines, candy, soda, and cards, either hockey, baseball and/or STAR WARS. When you first entered this magic kingdom, the bell on the door would welcome all visitors and alert Dennis, the owner who was perched high above where the prescriptions were filled. Dennis always reminded of me of St. Louis Cardinals first baseman Keith Hernandez, and I may have called him Keith once or twice...not a bad thing. Sadly, I remember being in Pigeons' and hearing on the radio that New York Yankees catcher Thurman Munson died in a plane crash. A lot of memories in that building.

The layout of the store is etched in my brain. I would walk about ten feet in and find the large magazine rack to the left with a small spinner rack for paperbacks. This area had an awesome ink and paper smell that made me always know that life was good, no matter what. After flipping through the comics on the base of the shelf I would stand up and look through some of the magazines on top of the fixture; STARLOG, BASEBALL DIGEST, CREEPY...but sometimes my eyes would accidently rise to the top shelf to see some of the girlie mags. Nothing too bad (those were behind the register. Stuff like TRUE DETECTIVE and VAMPIRELLA would catch my eye, but it would only be a quick look. I wasn't a perv, and Dennis knew my parents, so I didn't wanna get caught and have him tell them I was a peeper. I would leave the rack, take a few steps, turn at the large floor vent, step on the creaky floorboard, and make my way toward the food counter (something I never saw before) and cash register with a showcase of cards and candy. But before I would get there I would always stop at the toy section that contained a small assortment of cool model kits and overpriced toys. Stuka dive bomber, Bell Huey Helicopter, and, for some reason, a SHOGUN WARRIORS kits; all model kits I wanted to buy and build one day. But I had to get the most with my three bucks. The delicious orange-smelling model glue tubes had to be purchased at the register by the food counter and asked for. I couldn't quite understand why it was behind the register but describing it now as delicious orange may have had something to do with it.

As I left Pigeons' with a bag full of purchases including comic books, baseball cards, and a few delicious Choco-diles, I noticed a strange glow coming from the top of Main Street heading toward the Elementary School. The glow looked like the poster for CLOSE ENCOUNTERS OF THE THIRD KIND, that even after seeing the movie still kinda scared me a little. There was a weird smell in the air, like burning hair and soap bubbles, but my curiosity got the best of me. It wasn't too dark yet, so I decided to take a walk up toward the glow to see what was causing the weird blue light.

"Maybe it's the carnival rides being tested in the church parking lot," I said to myself, unwrapping one of the Choco-diles and eating the chocolate off first, exposing just a plain Twinkie underneath.

As I started to get a little closer, walking up the hill towards St. Catherine's Church, the odd smell got stronger and stranger. Since I suffered from seasonal allergies and ever-clogging sinuses, my sense of smell was always a little off to begin with, but this pungent scent hit me like a ton of black LEGO bricks. It was so strong I could taste it over my Hostess snack!

"Ewwww, it smells like a pile of burning Filet-O-Fish and Crest toothpaste," I said to myself pinching my nose closed with no other words to describe it.

I got up to the fork in the road with the church in the middle of it, but I decided it was getting dark and kind of late. I also realized I told my parents I was just going to Pigeon's, so I started to hightail it back home carefully avoiding Tommy's Bar and Grille on Main Street. I was told that any little kids walking by would get beat up in there and I didn't want to get beat up by drunk men looking for trouble.

"What was that color?" I kept saying to myself, "and what was that fishy smell?" I chalked it up to a new town and new town smells. My old town of Hampden had its share of smells, but nothing that didn't come out of a horse, pig, or cow.

This kept playing over and over in my mind. As I lay in bed listening to the magic of WINGS GREATEST, I could see the electric-blue glow in the distance filtering through my semi-closed blinds. Did anyone else think this was a little *off*? Sure, every once in a while, we got a whiff of the burning dump at the top of North

Road, and even the slime- covered Broad Brook Pond, and they didn't ever whiff that bad. I could still smell and taste that strange odor and then it dawned on me…THE OCEAN! Like a Texas Instruments Little Professor, I began to calculate everything that was going on. I reached under my bed and pulled out my Trapper Keeper, opened the no-spill pockets, and pulled out the plans I drew up in case of emergency, like a Russian Invasion or crazy people from New York sneaking into Connecticut like I heard they tried to do in 1977 during the New York Blackout…and this was an emergency! But before I could do anything or put plans to paper, I fell asleep.

With the weekend now upon us, me and my friends' thoughts were all about the Broad Brook Carnival and the fun we were going to have, especially since our parents would let us go without adult supervision. "How much trouble can you get into at the BBC?" my mom said. Friday night was great because you would see friends you haven't seen since school ended a month earlier despite living only a few miles from them. But Saturday night belonged to the amazing precision of those marching in the parade, school bands, volunteer firemen, and their awesome fire trucks.

The Mill Pond Crew tried our luck at all three of the games of skill and chance provided at the carnival. We all were losers except for Tommy, my friend who was visiting from Springfield. Tommy was a comic book collector friend of mine who I met at Treasure Island in Baystate West just before I moved to Connecticut. With skill and steady aim, Tommy won; squirting water into a clown's mouth, inflating and then popping a balloon on the clown's head.

"You sure are good with a gun," I told him, admiring his skill. "When you grow up you should join the army or become a policeman like John and Ponch from ChiPs." Tommy just smiled and collected his prize, a Molly Hatchet mirror in a cardboard sleeve. Cool as the mirror was it certainly wasn't worth the $11.75 he spent to win it, but hey, he won it. Unfortunately, Tommy dropped his prize in the Port-O-Potty while going to the bathroom. Tommy had mad skills but unzipping and holding a mirror in the bathroom wasn't one of them.

I purchased a homemade Carmel Apple and had to be very careful eating it. I only had a few months to go wearing my braces and I was told one of these babies would not only get caught in my braces but maybe pull them right off my teeth! Of course, I didn't believe that could ever happen, but there was still some care and caution in my biting and chewing.

Wanting to get a better view of the parade heading down Main Street, Kevin and I jumped on the shaky Ferris Wheel to see all the action from above. As we waited in line, I could still smell that weird fishy toothpaste smell from the night before. Standing in front of us to get on the wheel was Kerry and her friend Sue who lived in the Windsorville section of East Windsor, a small town within another small town. I only knew Sue a little bit because I saw her last year at school delivering a film projector to my homeroom so we could watch a dumb filmstrip about photosynthesis. After two minutes of awkward greetings, Kerry and her friend Sue who lived in the Windsorville section of East Windsor, a small town within another small town. I only knew Sue a little bit because I saw her last year at school delivering a film projector to my homeroom so we could watch a dumb filmstrip about photosynthesis. After two minutes of awkward greetings, Kerry mentioned that the air smelled a bit like Crest toothpaste and our drinking water, which was fluorinated and tasted crappy. As soon as she said that I perked up a bit realizing she just gave me a clue for unraveling this mystery.

"You're right," I said with a quizzical look on my face. That was it. All I said. I was still incredibly shy around girls and Kerry and Sue were both very cute, so that brought out even more shyness.

Before I moved to Broad Brook, I lived on my grandparent's farm in a little place called Hampden, Massachusetts. The farm was over 60 acres. It was an amazing place to grow up and have all sorts of adventures. The farm had horses, some pigs, a few geese, and a pony named Dutch that almost brought on my demise and created a fear of horses that never went away. The negative part of so much land to play on was that my school friends lived farther away and couldn't just walk over to play. This meant that I spent most of the time being an army of one or just playing with my G.I. Joes alone in the vast wilderness. We got our water from a well, straight from the ground. I never understood how a huge, covered hole gave us all that water...but it did, and I accepted that. Now, my water came from a big tower that smelled and tasted funny like I was drinking toothpaste. My first few months of drinking my new water I got sick from it, and it took me about six months to get used to the smell and taste of it. But not Sue.

"My house has well water and when it rains it gets all muddy," she said. Yuck! Something was definitely going on here and it had to do with this fluoride and fishy smell! Sadly, that was all I had as far as information. I didn't even have enough to make a fun Schoolhouse Rock-style song and rhyme with it... but I sure tried.

From high atop the Ferris Wheel, Kevin and I could see the whole length of the parade and not just the part that was going by us. Granted, when our basket was at the bottom close to the ground, we couldn't see anything, so it may not have been the best of plans. School bands, the local baseball and softball teams, Cub Scouts, Boy Scouts, Brownies, Girl Scouts…they all marched right down Main Street and took a right at the end and dispersed off of Enfield Street by the grass parking lots. One of the things we were waiting for was the bright red and shiny trucks belonging to the "first in action" Broad Brook Volunteer Fire Department, complete with sirens-a-blazing. Because of the action and adventure TV series, EMERGENCY, I was still a little fascinated by fire trucks and fire dudes, so I was still in awe when they drove by, but what ten-year-old isn't?

Usually, the fire trucks and some cool-looking old cars from the 1950s would be at the end of the parade, but there was something else a little further down the road…a bonus parade, I thought! Despite the fact that the parade should be over, it seemed like something else was coming up the road. From a distance you could hear a weird marching sound, almost a slapping sound on the pavement, and that strange blue glow from last night was now coming up the street toward the carnival grounds.

"I thought the parade was over," Kevin asked looking over toward the oncoming unknown, "but I think something else is coming." With that I knew something was seriously wrong and knew we had to get off the Wheel.

"Dude, we have got to get off this ride," I yelled to Kevin as I positioned myself to leap out of the moving carriage. Before I could spring into action and possibly break my leg, the ride just ended, and Kevin and I got out the right way…with a smelly, toothless carny opening the bar and telling us to get out in a not-so-nice tone and with a few swear words! Suddenly the jovial carnival atmosphere turned to fear and panic as people began screaming and running away from what was coming up the street.

Fearing the onslaught of a thousand panicky humans, I ran across the field to the now-vacant cotton candy booth and hid in the fetal position under a box of those white handle cone things. All around me, there was screaming and explosions. Between the slats in the booth, I could see men, women, and children with pure terror in their eyes and I knew I had to get out of here. Something scary was coming up the street toward us and the people in their wake were… well, I don't exactly know what was happening. I decided to use my incredible (and award-winning) 50-yard dash super-speed ability and make my way home as fast as I could, leaving Kevin somewhere like a very un-loyal friend.

The ground shook with explosion after earth-shattering explosion, so as I tried to run I could feel my Converse All Stars (complete with no traction at all) slipping with every shimmy and shake. Then, as I went to turn a corner near the field, I could hear scurrying coming toward me. When I moved to see what it was, I was both shocked and horrified…an Aquatic Ape!?!? This thing was as tall as a high school kid and looked like they do in the comic book ads… but huge! There were hundreds of them just destroying things and hurting anyone that got in their way. I first thought this was just a horrible dream or hallucination caused by model glue and rubber cement fumes, but I knew in my heart it wasn't a dream. This was all too real.

I could see what they were doing but didn't quite know how. From out of their hands would come these balls of clear, yellow energy. They would close their hands together like they were packing a snowball and when they pulled them apart, they had a glowing orb that must have contained explosives of some kind. When they threw them, whatever it hit would just blow up!

Trying to escape these imposing figures, I hid in some bushes to get a better look at these things and see what was actually going on. They were HUGE…I mean *really* tall! They stood about 6 1/2 feet tall from their flippery webbed feet all the way to the red balls on the antennae/crown thing on the top of their heads. Their skin was a light blue, covered in gills and they had big toothy white grins on their faces. Even when they were destroying stuff or hurting people, they just smiled. They also had long tails that swayed back and forth when they walked or ran. THAT was creepy.

"This is a bloody nightmare!" I yelled to myself, clenching my fists, and not quite knowing what to do. Everywhere I looked there were these smiling Aquatic Apes, just destroying the carnival and my town. Some of them were chasing people and cornering them, some were dragging folks into the center of the field across the street, and some were just standing over bodies, smiling, and laughing. No one fought back at all, and who could blame them? The only resistance they encountered was Ole Beau, the cool-looking dog with one blue and one brown eye. Although I was terrified of dogs (as well as horses), Beau was super-cool looking, especially when he dragged his owner by his leash due to his sheer strength and size. This insanity went on for about a half-hour or so and then, without any warning…the attack just stopped, and they were all gone.

When I was able to get up and walk around, I was horrified by what I saw. The scene looked like the ice of the Springfield Civic Center following a hockey brawl between the Springfield Indians and the rival New Haven Nighthawks, with stuff everywhere like a garage sale gone amok. Some people were wandering around in a mute shock while others lay on the ground crying and confused as cotton candy blew around like delicious tumbleweeds. Realizing I needed to get home quickly, I ran down Main Street, which now looked like Godzilla had just passed through. Houses were on fire, cars were overturned, and I passed by an older guy on his knees near a pile of burning books.

"Those monsters destroyed the library," he yelled. "All the books, the microfiche, the Dewy Decimal System file things…*everything* is in ruins!" I walked by and stared at him, sad and incredibly shocked...because, to be honest, I didn't even know Broad Brook had a library. But there it was, now a small smoldering pile of ash, stampers, index cards, and rubber bands.

I was a little worried as I got near Pigeon's, praying it wasn't destroyed. A few seconds later I was reassured to see that the building was untouched, and the comic books inside were safe. Now, I began to worry about my family.

I walked home over the bridge and past the waterfall that seemed to be flowing with even more force than normal. It was at that point I saw the damage seemed to be confined to the part of Main Street on the other side of the bridge up to the pizza shop. The Broad Brook Opera House and post office seemed to be untouched, meaning my part of town might be safe from the onslaught. The smell from the day before got a little stronger and the blueish glow was much brighter than it was the previous night, making the center of town illuminated with that crazy color.

I made it home a little before 11:00 PM, a few minutes later than I was told to be home, and all the way there I was fighting the mental images of my family being beat up by Aquatic Apes, seeing them rip up my growing comic book collection, or destroying my impressive display of Star Wars toys. I ran across the lawn, jumped down the slight embankment, onto the porch, and almost went through our glass front door. I pulled it open and almost off its hinges, then yelled for my parents who answered me from the kitchen.

When I got into view, my dad smiled and said, "Wow, we could hear the fireworks from here! Very impressive."

I was out of breath from the mad dash for safety but began to tell them everything that just happened in full, clear, and almost photographic details. The looks on my parents faces told me that they didn't understand a word I babbled out at a million miles an hour. I wasn't as clear as I thought with my words.

"Ummm…and these things….and…they blew up things…and (panting)…they did…the big Aquatic Apes...came to the….fried dough….fire balls (explosion noise with full hand gesture)…screaming!" In that entire tirade the only thing that my parents heard me say was, "Oh, yeah, and I saw Meredith and her friends all smoking drugs!" Shocked at their out-of-control child (who they began to think was the one on drugs), my mother told me to stop talking, gave me a big hug, and said to get cleaned before bed.

Not much later, as I sat in bed looking at the ceiling full of model airplanes, now all blueish from the weird light, I could hear my dad coming up the stairs. He took a right at the top and came into my room carrying my cat, Meinu.

"You okay?" he asked me, knowing I was really upset about something. I nodded yes as he put the Siamese cat under my arm as he did almost every night since I was 5. "All the TV channels are off the air right now, so we'll just have to see what the Hartford Courant reports in the Sunday edition."

"The morning?" I thought. After what I saw a few hours ago I wasn't sure we were even going to survive the night.

Of course, I didn't sleep a wink. I heard sirens in the distance going up and down the streets, voices sounding like they were using a Mr. Microphone from Ronco. I think they were talking about all the destruction.

Like clockwork the next morning my pal David delivered the big fat Sunday edition of the Hartford Courant. Instead of the headline reading AQUATIC APES ATTACK SMALL TOWN CARNIVAL, it was something about Governor Ella Grasso possibly running for vice president and her doing something good for someone. Was there a cover-up or conspiracy going on and was the Governor now involved? Due to my dad's Native American heritage, he didn't trust the government too much and was always suspicious of the press, except for Paul Harvey. I frantically flipped through the entire newspaper, my hands now black with ink smudges, but I couldn't find any mention of the previous night's events. I did read that the Montreal Expos won with Gary Carter and Warren Cromarte hitting dingers! What I did find, hidden in the paper within the Caldor circular was an envelope, addressed to me personally! I loved Caldors, the best store ever, and someone knew this! Was it that teenager Kenny I met who would put aside toys for me and loved baseball? I needed to read on!

"Dear Matt! I'm hoping that as you read this letter it isn't already too late and the Aquatic Apes haven't begun their calculated and precise attacks on humanity. If not, then it will only be a matter of time before they strike." Why am I getting this letter? "The reason you are getting this letter is simple. It is your brilliant mind and spending habits that I think make you a valuable ally in this all-important fight! We see how much money you have spent on comic books in the past few years as well as how many times you have seen STAR WARS, not to mention the hours of quality television you watch like BATTLESTAR GALACTICA and all the merchandise you purchase from comic books. Because of this we know you think like a warrior!"

Who is *we?* And why are you thinking about me? And was David involved? He was always way smarter than me.

So far so good! I was hanging on every word of this and had seen STAR WARS five times in the theater already. I was also glad that I filled out all those surveys in the comic books, asking all those personal but cool questions, and now it was finally paying off. I knew being a Nielson Family would one day pay off too, especially since I filled out all my family's logbooks. There was a reason so many crappy TV shows like SUPERTRAIN lasted longer than they should have, and that was all me. I continued to read...

"This is going to be a long hard-fought war and you have proven to be a survivor already! There will be a point when we need to sit back, strategize, and wait for our turn, but I know you will not be just one of the soldiers in the trenches. You will be a true leader in the struggle for freedom. I would have you reference the 204 Revolutionary War Soldiers you sent away for back in 1975. Those brave, blue soldiers rebelled against the tyranny and physical might of the red soldiers! The lessons you learned will be invaluable in this fight, no matter the odds. When you set up your soldiers you knew there were 24 Native and 12 Hessian troops helping the red soldiers, and you knew the blue soldiers had guts, moxy, and desire to win. This is how you will lead, fight, and help win this war for our survival."

UH-OH! If this was the reason I was selected for whatever this was, the entire human race is in serious trouble! When I 'ordered' the 204 Revolutionary War Soldiers a few years back, it asked for a check, and, since I didn't know high finance, or any finance other than the cash in my pocket, I asked for help. When filling out the coupon and stuffing it in an envelope, my mother just wrote on a piece of paper her name, $1.98, and the word "check." She told a 6-year-old me desperate for these toys that this was what a check was, and in six to eight weeks I would have my toys. That was three long and lonely years ago, not to mention three moves, and I was still waiting. I can remember the words as she wrote the "check" in anger. "Would it kill you if you didn't have these soldiers?" Now it looks like it may have killed us all. But I continued to read…

"So please be diligent, await more letters, and read every issue of GRIT for more of my reports. If you haven't done so yet, start selling American Seeds! As you will see in the ad, everyone wants American Seeds and you can earn some fantastic prizes like an archery set, a tent, and a complete fishing kit. The impending invasion of the Aquatic Apes may have begun in the pages of comic books, but the revolution will be fought with these fantastic prizes! Remember, Matt, send no money. They trust you!"

The letter was signed once again by this Jeff guy who was becoming a mystery wrapped in another mystery. Now since an attack had already happened just the night before, I knew this was no joke. I needed to start packing emergency supplies right away since food may become scarce and I didn't want to go hungry. I emptied out my Uncle Sam piggy bank and asked my dad to take me to Caldors or even my second choice, Zayre, both in Enfield, but he was a strict Blue Law kind of guy. This meant that there would be no shopping on Sunday, only church, the odd tag sales, and flea markets. My all-important supply run would have to wait, but it gave me more time to prepare what I would actually need to survive.

I had a serious plan of what would be needed if I had to go without food. For those cold nights or the entire winter season if the war went on too long, I would need foods like Flamesuckers candy and Lipton Giggle Noodle Soup to keep warm. I would also need a couple of big bottles of Mello Yello, but my smartest acquisition would be Marathon Bars. After all, the commercial does promise that they would last "a long, long time" and I would probably need that, not knowing the difference between advertising and a literal long time. Despite my braces and the world-famous spider egg controversy, a few packs of Bubble Yum gum were definitely a necessity. How did spider eggs even get into the gum factory? But who cared if there were spider eggs in the gum. Those pieces were soft and juicy and quite flavorful!

My gum budget would need to be stretched to include a pack or two of Bubble Fudge just to see if it's as bad as it sounds. *Chewing* chocolate? And for the campfires I would have a couple tins of Jiffy Pop ready. You never know when you're going to want 'pop' corn during the end of the world.

We would all have to make sacrifices, but my cereal eating would never be a victim. To make it through the long haul, I would get a lot of Kellogg's Jumbo assortment; 18 individual boxes of cereal that came in their own bowls. Sure, I would have to eat a Raisin Bran or Corn Flakes, but desperate times! My friend Joe from New York used to call it winning the lottery if you got doubles of one of the cool ones like Corn Pops, Sugar Smacks, or Apple Jacks. Joe was so smart but wait, what do I do about *milk?* Get a couple of boxes of this powdered milk! Specifically, Milkman Milk, featuring a "kiss of cream." Getting water would be easy. I would just go to the cleanest part of Broad Brook Pond and scoop out a cup or two as needed. What you can't see can't hurt you, right? *Science!*

Seeing how concerned and freaked out I was, my dad broke his own rule and took me to the closest town we could get to, Rockville, just a few miles up the street to the east. Sitting in his beat-up green Ford pickup truck at one of the traffic lights, my dad asked me exactly what had happened the night before, like he was really concerned. I repeated everything I saw much clearer, including my sister and her friends smoking all those drugs, hoping to get her in trouble. We flipped around the radio dial of the truck looking for any news, but we didn't hear anything other than Captain and Tennille, a lot of disco, and other hits of the day that I would come to appreciate more and more as time went on. Oddly, nothing was said about any Aquatic Ape attacks. But soon enough, the news, whether it was the radio, newspapers, or television, would be reporting this invasion and the hostile takeover by the smiling, blue devils. We would find out by word of mouth that last night's scenario had taken place in a few Connecticut towns like New Haven, Meriden, and a few others I never even heard of.

Things were getting really serious, very real, and incredibly scary.

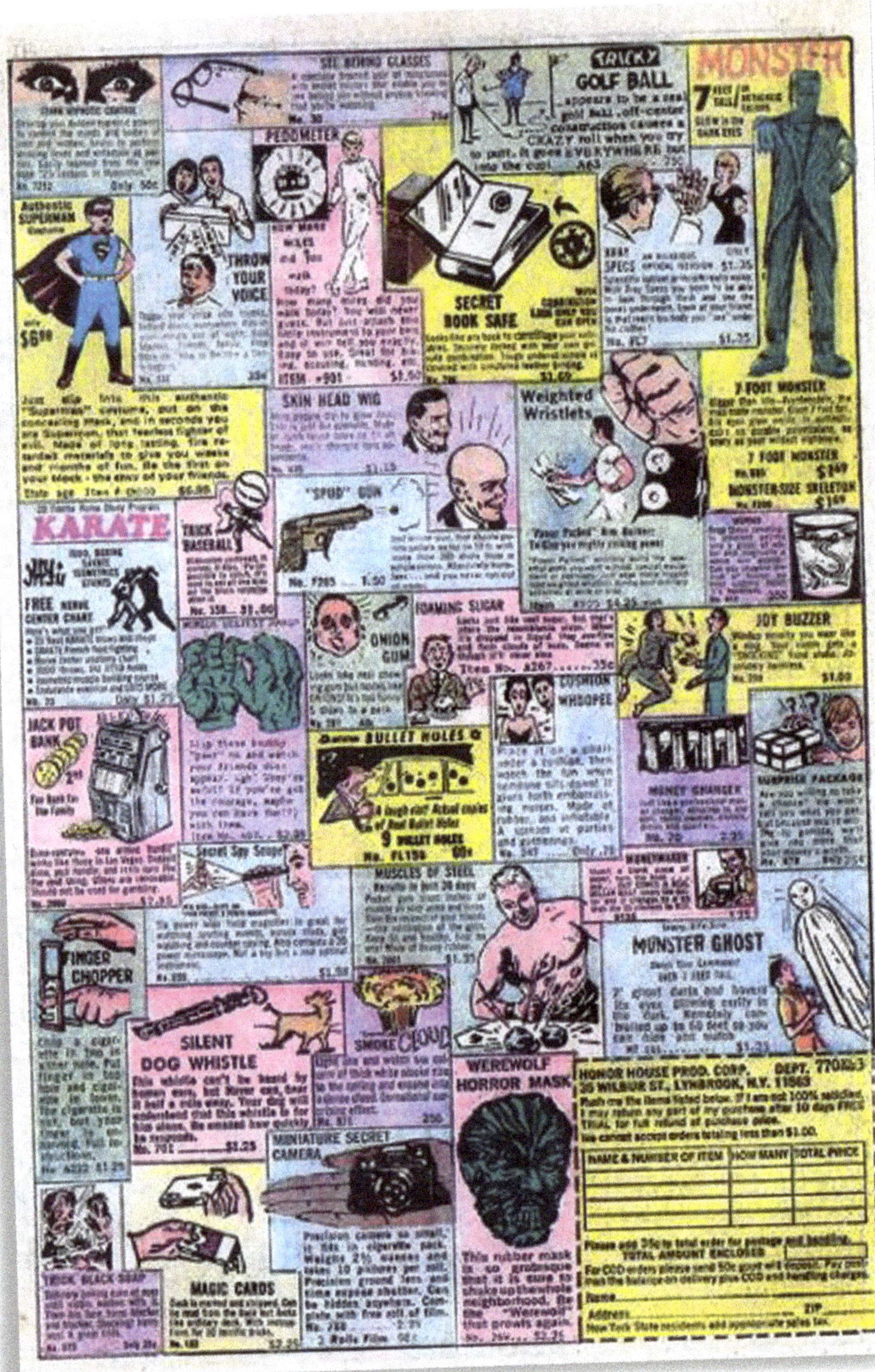

SEE BEHIND GLASSES
GOLF BALL
MONSTER
PEDOMETER
THROW YOUR VOICE
SECRET BOOK SAFE
X-RAY SPECS
Authentic SUPERMAN Costume
$6.00
SKIN HEAD WIG
Weighted Wristlets
7 FOOT MONSTER
MONSTER-SIZE SKELETON
KARATE
TRICK BASEBALL
"SPUD" GUN
FOAMING SUGAR
ONION GUM
JOY BUZZER
JACK POT BANK
CUSHION WHOOPEE
BULLET HOLES
MONEY CHANGER
SURPRISE PACKAGE
MUSCLES OF STEEL
FINGER CHOPPER
MONSTER GHOST
SILENT DOG WHISTLE
SMOKE CLOUD
WEREWOLF HORROR MASK
MINIATURE SECRET CAMERA
MAGIC CARDS
HONOR HOUSE PROD. CORP.   DEPT. 770183
35 WILBUR ST., LYNBROOK, N.Y. 11563
NAME & NUMBER OF ITEM   HOW MANY   TOTAL PRICE
TOTAL AMOUNT ENCLOSED
Name
Address   ZIP
New York State residents add appropriate sales tax.

hair
Teeth
Best of Luck to the Class of "79"
From PIGEON'S PHARMACY
Main St.   Broad Brook
OPERA HOUSE
TOMMY'S
RESTAURANT
FINE FOODS
COCKTAILS
CARNIVAL

CHAPTER THREE
"Somewhere In The Night"

As my dad and I made our way back home with the much-needed supplies (some of which I ate on the way) we came back the long way to see if we could drive by the carnival grounds. Here, my dad would see the destruction and believe what I was telling him. As our truck got closer, I was shocked to see that they were setting up the rides and booths again, getting ready for another night of carnival action and fun. It puzzled me that, despite the fact that people were injured and maybe even killed last night, things were just going on as normal, like nothing ever happened...and something happened! As we turned down Main Street, I could see a bunch of cool TV cameras following around some well-dressed older dudes, a sight you don't see every day. As I peered out the open window like a dog (possibly with my tongue hanging out), I got all excited!

"Holy cow," I yelled to my dad, "that's the whole Action News team right here in Broad Brook!" If anyone would get to the bottom of this crazy thing, I thought, it would be Channel 8. They were the *best!*

Seeing people that I see on TV was a cool thing, especially for a young kid in the 1970s. I remember seeing Super Don, a curly-haired guy who dressed in a Superman suit and sold furniture, and I *freaked* out as my parents tried to buy a couch! This guy was real famous...granted, small market and local famous, but famous nonetheless!

When we got home, I took everything I hadn't eaten, put them into a green backpack, and left it by the front door just in case I needed to spring into action. At 5 PM I sat in front of the television waiting to hear the Action News team expose this amazing cover-up and stop the carnival to prevent last night's insanity from happening all over again. As the report began, I was so excited to see the familiar sights and people I knew, flashing on my TV screen. The narrative went on to tell a very watered-down version of the events that I saw firsthand. There was no mention of Aquatic Apes, but the incident was reported as mass hysteria caused by fumes from the nearby dump fire, creating a collective hallucination at the exact same time a gang of out-of-town hoodlums caused damage.

"WHAT the heck," I yelled! "They sure were out of towners...they were friggin' Aquatic Apes!"

Then, almost on cue, the members of the Carnival Committee appeared together, all smiling really weird, with a balding, heavyset guy in a plaid jacket a size too small stepping up to the microphone.

"Good afternoon, good people of Broad Brook," said the committee spokesman Mr. Briette into the camera. "What happened last night at our carnival has been drastically exaggerated, and I can assure you all that the Broad Brook Carnival is a safe place for the friends and families of this wonderful community to enjoy themselves. Have fun, don't worry about Aquatic, ummmm …I mean gangs of troublemakers and hooligans from other towns. We will have extra police on hand to keep any trouble from happening again, and free fried dough for everyone with a limit of one per customer…and you have to pay for a topping."

Holy Cow! This Mr. Briette guy knows!!! He knows about the Aquatic Apes and he's covering it all up like the Mayor in JAWS telling everyone the beach is safe! Now if I learned three important life lessons from the movie JAWS, it's not to go swimming naked at night, if you cut a shark open, you'll find a license plate in their stomach, and the most important of all…if the mayor or town official says it's okay to swim following a shark attack then plan on a lot of body bags and a bigger boat. Emotions began to swell inside me and I knew I couldn't let whatever happened last night play itself out again. I knew I needed to act. I had to go to the press myself, and by the press I meant David, the local paperboy who happened to be way smarter than I was.

Running to Dave's apartment building at breakneck speed I found out that he had already left for the carnival. His apartment building was far from my town-house and his apartment was on the top floor. What a waste of a trip! As I walked down Depot Street, I could hear the music and smell the fried dough. I arrived a little out of breath and noticed a commotion around the committee members, with concerned townsfolk attacking them with question after question.

"Is our town safe?" yelled a woman holding a very young child with concern in her eyes.

"Are there really Aquatic Apes running loose in Broad Brook?" an older gentleman asked, waving his finger at the council, "and, if so, what is a dang-gummed Aquatic Ape?!"

"How do I get my free fried dough?" my pal Jon asked. I knew where his priorities were.

Raising his hands like a Sunday preacher ready to give a sermon, Mr. Briette, cleaning his thick glasses with a rag, got control of the growing and somewhat unruly crowd of three people. "Good people," he started as his forehead began to perspire, "I know you are all a little scared right now, but I have been assured that what happened here last night *can't* and *won't* happen again. We have added extra security from bringing in one more police officer to keep things in order. This carnival will continue because we can't show fear in the face of adversity, not to mention this carnival injects about $326 into the local economy, so the show *must* and *will* go on." Like lemmings, everyone nodded and seemed reassured. "So please go and enjoy the great rides, some cotton candy, and some delicious, healthy, *free* fried dough, limit one per customer." And with that everyone, all three of them, just left.

I didn't quite know what to think. Why were they giving everyone free fried dough? Was there something in it to make us obey? Was it going to slow us down so we couldn't run? At my young age I did understand that adults didn't just lie about things, and that we had to trust them, but something didn't seem quite right here. If I learned anything from JAWS 2 it was that when evil sharks attack, they attack again and possibly again and again, even if you blow them up or electrocute them!

Needing to excuse myself from this potential bloodbath I wandered up the other end of Main Street to St. Catherine's Church, a big white beacon of hope that was the only thing in the area which didn't seem to be covered in that strange blue light. Granted, the last few times I was inside the church it was for confession, and, to be honest, it didn't go that well for me. This time was much different. I needed to be in God's house, or at least his weekend home in Broad Brook. As I got a little closer, I could see there were already a collection of people inside, more than during any Saturday Evening service. I noticed the door was open so I quietly walked in and sat in the far back pew to the left. I reached into my bag, pulled out one of my Marathon Bars, and spent a little bit of time talkin' to the big guy. As I prayed, I became distracted by all the stained glassed windows featuring Jesus, lambs, and crowds of people. But then my attention was drawn outside to a small rumble and some screaming in the distance. I didn't want to move so I just laid down in the pew and hid from the world and the horrors I knew were happening just down the street. Then, possibly from all the excitement of the last few days, I fell asleep.

A few hours later I woke up to a building now packed with people, hundreds of them, all looking scared and a little worse for wear. Some had blood or cherry Italian ice juice on them, their clothes were ripped and dirty, babies were crying, and everyone smelled like smoke, toothpaste, and fish.

"What happened?" I asked the man sitting next to me who looked to be in serious shock. He didn't answer, just stared ahead, motionless, mumbling to himself. As I started to get up, I saw a young girl sitting in front of me who I didn't recognize. Not only was she wearing a Princess Leia t-shirt, but she also had her hair in the very tight and stylish Princess Leia buns. I could see she was drawing on a pad of paper, and, of course, I wanted to see what it was. She stopped working and looked up at me, adjusting her very stylish glasses.

"Hi, I'm Karen," she said to me, "Do you like STAR WARS, too?" I told her I *loved* STAR WARS, and, with that answer, she gave me a picture she was working on of Luke Skywalker fighting Darth Vader with awesome light saber action! And she even got the light saber colors right, too.

"This picture is great", I told her admiring her handiwork. "Do you live around here?"

"No," she told me. "My family and I are here from New Hampshire and were visiting the Trolley Museum when the Aquatic Apes attacked the train. Then we ended up here." Bad time to visit Broad Brook indeed!

I left the sacred grounds of the church and walked down the eerily quiet and empty street. I was thinking I should go back home and check in with my family, but my curiosity was a little stronger than my loyalty to family. In times like this I drew on the strength of Action Jackson and his team, who would put their duty before their family or themselves. "DO OR DARE, HE'S EVERYWHERE" the box read… and that would be me, minus the cool baby blue jumpsuit. Was it me wanting to be part of the greater good or morbid curiosity drawing me back to the battlefield that was once the carnival?

As I kept walking closer and closer under flickering streetlights, I expected to see barricades, fire trucks, and police all over the place, but there was nothing. Nothing at all. Something different was happening. I knew that the best way to get to the carnival grounds undetected was to get out of the open and sneak there, cutting across backyards along Main Street and the pond. A few times I got too close and stepped in the nasty river muck and would once or twice pull out a shoeless foot, so that slowed me down a bit, but I was now getting closer… oh so much closer.

In the large clearing by the back of the field I could see a lot of confusion and commotion going on. Then I saw it! There were about seventy-five Aquatic Apes all around the area doing various things. Now I could confirm this wasn't part of any mass hallucinations. I knew exactly what I was seeing. Some of the Aquatic Apes were putting up fences across the street to pen in their captive humans. The material for the fences was made from whatever the apes would spit into their webbed hands, working it into a weird, clear, sticky-looking thingy. They would then use that to make something that looked like fence wire that, when connected with other pieces, would create a stockade. I could see some of the town officials huddled together in the presence of a couple of larger Aquatic Apes who were obviously the ones in charge. The town officials were powerless and defeated. We all were. It was the Dawn of the Aquatic Apes.

As amazing a physical and scary presence that these creatures were, I couldn't help but chuckle to myself on how their voices sounded. Their vocal tone was very high-pitched and almost bubbly in its inflection, sounding like Barry Gibb of the Bee Gees singing into a glass of water, but certainly not as cool. From my vantage point under the trees, I could see that these monsters were organized… very organized. And they kept on coming, arriving every few minutes from every direction…down Main Street, up North Road, from Enfield Street…more and more apes. Some were bigger and meaner than others, but all wearing those silly, toothy smiles. When they marched, they stayed in perfect formation with their webbed feet slapping on the pavement like wet flippers on a pool deck. The more that arrived the more fearful I became, fearful of my future, for my family, and everything that I knew and loved. Everything was changing and certainly not for the better.

For the next hour I watched the Aquatic Apes put a systematic plan in place.

They were taking many of the captive humans into their newly made stockades. They would grab a random person, force their eyes open, and, to me, appeared to be separating their captives by eye color. Why eye color, and which ones would be the *wrong* color? If they were going to force them to work, I would think that they would take the most physical ones. Certain people were let go while others were forced into the pens. In the middle of the field, humans were forced to clear all the carnival items away, clearing it for something. I wasn't sure I wanted to know what for. What happened next was something right out of…well, something pretty crazy looking. About thirty Aquatic Apes broke ranks and went to the clearing to spit (again with the spitting!) out this phlegmy, brown-looking gooey substance that looked like my spit after I ate a Sugar Daddy. As it began to collect in a big pile (from all the spitting) other Aquatic Apes came over. They were much smaller and a bit chunkier than the other ones, using their tails to slap into shape the piles of goo until they began to take the form of a giant castle…and it was just like one you'd find at the bottom of a fish tank or in the back of the ad in the comic books for Aquatic Apes. This was all pretty scary but also quite impressive!

Thinking of Sugar Daddy's, I started to get a little hungry and knew I needed to get back home, so I started to slink away. Before I did, I could see my friend Kerry in one of the holding pens and looking very sad. Like George Lazenby as James Bond, I slinked (again with the slinking!) over on my belly to get closer to her location. I whisper-yelled her name a few dozen times until she finally saw me and waved. Then I got up, slinked (I'm very good at slinking) across the street, and went up to her.

"Hey", I said to her, nodding like everything was cool, or at least that I was cool. Standing next to her was Laura, our mutual friend who didn't look so happy. "Why are you guys in there?" I asked curiously.

"From what I could understand, it's because we have blue eyes." I looked at Laura's eyes to discover she had blue eyes as well. Sad, I never noticed before, but I don't normally look into people's eyes due to my shyness issues.

"That sucks," I told them, trying to see if I could move the bars of this ape-made prison. Sadly, I couldn't even get it to budge. I told the two of them that I would be back with help as soon as I could and then I left, telling them I had to get home. "After my Swanson TV dinner I'll be back," I told them…and I meant it! I was gonna have a Swanson TV dinner.

In case I was followed, I snuck back to my house and came in the back way from behind the townhouses. It was a bit muddier and took longer going through the cow fields, but I thought it was a much safer path to follow, even in the dark. As I got closer to 5-F, I noticed that most of the cars in the lots were gone. The townhouses and apartments were all empty, too. As I crept up to my door, I saw a note flapping in the breeze just below the peep hole. I carefully took it town and walked into my house. My empty house. I went to the table, sat down, and began to read the note.

Dear Matt,

   By now you have probably noticed that the house is empty and we are all gone. Your mother and I thought it was best to take your sister and Meinu and sneak across the border to Massachusetts, which as of now is a safe and free zone. I know your talk of Aquatic Apes growing big and attacking people is true, so we had to leave....Wow! Interesting that my parents just left a ten-year-old kid all alone...bet it was my sister's idea. I read on… You are probably feeling like we abandoned you (mmm-hm) and are wondering why we didn't wait for you. After much heartbreaking discussion your mother and I realized that you could do much more good fighting the Aquatic Apes than running away and hiding with us. Sure, you are our child, and we love you but...BUT? What "but" could there be?…but you belong to the world now! Humanity needs you more than we need a son right now. I can see you leading humanity in its most desperate time like Charlton Heston in PLANET OF THE APES or Obi-Wan Kenobi in STAR WARS. ...Okay, dad, these are not very good examples because they both died, but I see what you are getting at in a roundabout way... Fate has chosen you to help deliver humanity from its darkest time and we can't think of a better choice! Your love of comic books, history, certain movies, and TV shows has finally paid off and can help you to lead the revolution against these horrific creatures. I have never been so proud of you, my son! Your birth certificate may say you are only ten, but today you are a man!

   Wow! I swear I could hear the BATTLESTAR GALACTICA theme playing in my head when I read that. I felt like a new person with a new purpose until I read the scribble at the bottom from my mom in green ink from her nursing pen.

   Hi Mattie, this is your mother. Just because you are out saving the world don't forget to brush your teeth extra good this week and remember no bubble gum from the STAR WARS and baseball cards. You still can't chew gum and you have an orthodontist appointment next Tuesday! And no soda!!! It eats away the cement holding the braces on. Love You! Mom

   Typical! I felt like Luke Skywalker still being treated like a little kid, needing to go to Tagge Station to pick up power converters. I bet Luke Skywalker's mom would have let him chew or even suck the sugar out of the gum if he had braces, but at least my dad thought I could do it, like Luke Skywalker's dad. I bet he was a pretty cool guy until Darth Vader betrayed and murdered him.

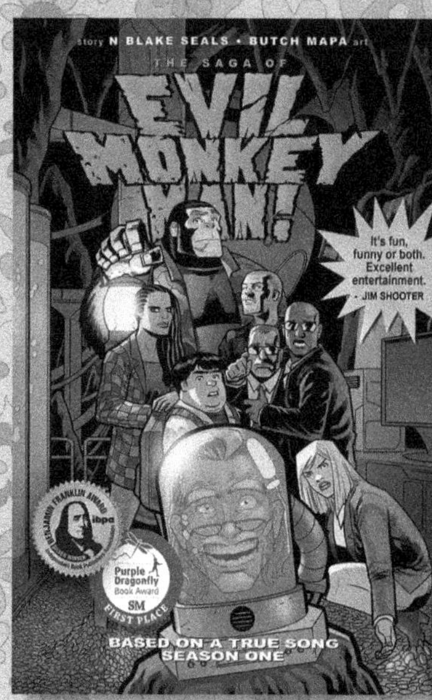

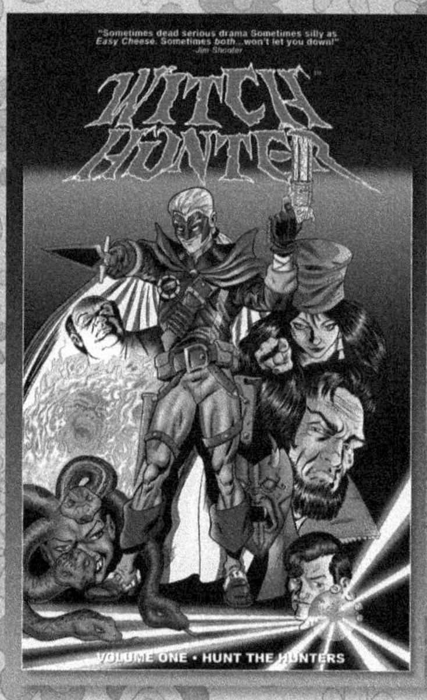

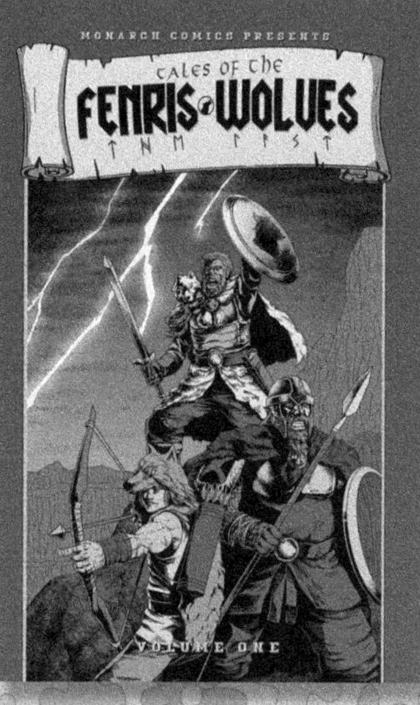

MONARCH COMICS

comic books the way they should be...fun!

monarchcomics.com

hair
teeth
SALE IS AT CALDOR
SPECTACULAR 2-DAY SAVINGS (FRIDAY & SATURDAY)
CALDOR
BOBCAT
CUB SCOUT
MY HOUSE — 5F TOWNHOUSE ROAD
PATH BY THE POND

CHAPTER FOUR
"Even Now"

It was a strange next couple of days to say the least. The thought that I was now a ten-year-old living alone was a fun idea and full of reckless possibilities for the first few hours, but then it got a little weird…and a little lonely. As outgoing as I have become once I got my stutter under control, I was a bit of a homebody and very regimented. I would have my play time, TV watching, and comic book reading on a schedule. During the summer, school wouldn't interfere with my life, so I would replace prison with swimming and more comic book reading.

I really missed my cat!

Broad Brook was a small town that had become a ghost town, with very few people around and not a lot on the streets. If you took a walk along Depot and Main Street, you would see the startling figures of Aquatic Apes walking around like they owned the place, because they *did,* without challenge. We were now a defeated race and now lived under their gross webbed feet. At least that fishy toothpaste smell was no longer filling the air, so that was good. For some odd reason, streets like Scantic and the lower part of Main were blocked off and heavily guarded by these Blueies, as I was now calling them, just not to their faces. Every time you came in contact with them you could feel them burning a hole in you with their crazy white eyes and creepy smiles.

Sadly, I would walk by people who were just crying and so upset because family members had gone missing and couldn't get any answers from anyone as to where they were taken. Now filling our small-town skyline was that crazy astle they were building at the fairgrounds, towering about 12 stories high. Using my high-powered binoculars that I got for only 75 cents. The comic book ad I bought them from claimed they could see up to eighteen miles. For the few miles I needed anyway, they did the trick. They folded up into a nice, neat package to bring anywhere, like a football game or bird watching.

"How did they build that castle thing so quick?" I thought out loud just staring at this mammoth structure standing as tall and imposing as the Broad Brook Water Tower. But, before I could move and walk away, I felt a flippered hand grab me by the shoulder. I got so startled my binoculars flew out of my hand eemingly in slow motion and dropped them into the pond next to me. I turned to see two Aquatic Apes right behind me, their height blocking out the sun.

"VHHHAAAAATTT ARE YOU LOOOKIIIINNNGGGG AT, HUMMMANNN?" one of the Apes asked me with a slight Germanic accent. So many times I thought how brave I would be in the face of real trouble. This time I just froze up stiff. Sadly, not my greatest moment.

"Ummmmm, well, I, uhhhhh...nothing," I mumbled, looking for a way to get out of this now growing scary situation.

"VVVVVVEEE TTTHHIIINNNKKK YOOUUUU NEEED TOOO COMMME VIIITTHHHH USSSS!" it ordered me. Okay, now I was terrified, like pee-my-pants terrified, not that I did or that I would ever admit if I did.

As I stood there pinned up against the rickety fence that kept people from falling into the pond, I could see a few more Aquatic Apes coming our way. I needed to do something to get out of this before I disappeared like so many others. I slid gently to the right a little bit in the only space there wasn't a Blueie standing. As the two looked over at the ones fast approaching, I sprang to action…and by sprang, I mean I ran like Montreal Expos fast guy Andre Dawson stealing a base.

Knowing they were right behind me I didn't need to turn around, but I could hear them. Because of their flippery webbed feet they couldn't run very fast and seemed useless on land. I was going to run just then, but was shaken by a scary horn sound, like someone blowing into a seashell only louder. Suddenly on the road in front of me I could see more Aquatic Apes approaching trying to cut me off.

Seeing the abandoned train tracks ahead, I decided to jump to the left of them so I would still be close to home, now called Home Base Alpha, like Moon Base Alpha from SPACE 1999! In times of trouble, everything had a code name! Since we would walk and run this path all the time, a small clearing was already cut into the tall, wild grass. There were two advantages I could think of being in here: one is that I knew every inch of these woods and tracks. I knew every hiding place, every shrub, every hollowed-out tree…everything. Number two is their flipper feet would get tripped up and tangled running on the train tracks and they probably wouldn't fit on the path either. So, I beat feet and tore down the tracks, running far enough to be able to hide and not worry about them seeing me, while I could still see them. I made it to a clearing about a quarter mile down the tracks, where there was a bunch of fallen trees that created a cool covering. It smelled like skunks and cigarettes but right now, as I slid inside of it, it smelled like safety.

Needing to talk this out with someone super smart, I looked over and could see the Aquatic Apes were beginning to scatter. Knowing they couldn't navigate the train tracks, I took my chances and scooted out of the woods, making it to T building. Here I could see David and get his advice on this matter. I walked up to the third floor and approached his apartment door where I could hear sobbing and a loud commotion. The door to David's apartment was open, and, judging by the wood shards on the carpet, it looked like it was forced open.

"They took them all…the whole family, gone," his elderly neighbor yelled in a European accent like she was blaming herself for what happened, "and I did nothing to stop them." What could she have *done?!*

David was gone. His mother, father, and sister, Belinda, were all gone, too! People were standing in the hall and in the stairwell trying to console the upset woman and work to figure out what had just happened. I started to leave the third floor and get outside fast because I felt a little shaken and now. I realized this was beginning to hit way too close to home. This wasn't a game! I would miss David, especially since he built model kits and would let me borrow paints when I needed them, plus, you know, the loss of human life and everything.

"*Pssst,* kid, hey, you!" a voice with a distinct, New York accent said, coming from the laundry room on the bottom floor of the apartment building. "You know they took your buddy and his family, right? The Aquatic Apes did this!" I carefully looked around the corner and saw a man there putting something into the dryer that wasn't clothes. I always loved hanging out in the laundry rooms because of the smell; a delicious cornucopia of Calgon, Dreft, and Bounce fabric softener sheets in a warm whiff of air. I walked into the somewhat damp room to find some guy who was much older, pretending to smoke a cigarette, dressed like Kolchak from the NIGHT STALKER, who was not letting me see his facial features at all. He reached out his hand and I shook it. "I'm Pincus! Alan Pincus!" He spoke quickly and barely stopped for pauses. "They took your friend because he was the press, *man!* History shows us that when an army invades or occupies a territory the first thing they do is disrupt the media and shut down all communications. Taking out your friend means no more newspapers will be delivered and the populace will be uninformed." He then shot me a serious look from under his hat. "You can now see how serious this is because his family is going to suffer as well."

As I started to walk away from this guy, he grabbed my arm and handed me a large manila envelope, told me to open it later, and not to go home because they may be watching me. I took it and ran back into the woods like the kid running from the Reading Is Fundamental (or R.I.F. for short) truck with a brand -new book; with speed and purpose. Instead of going right home, I followed the train tracks in the opposite direction toward the source of all the trouble. About a mile up the tracks, I saw one of my regular hideouts. I called this particular one Sanctuary, named after the place 'Runners' ran to in LOGAN'S RUN. When you regularly walk the tracks like I do, you always need a place to hide in a pinch in case big kids are on the same path as you, like Roscoe the town bully. Sanctuary had helped me so many times to avoid any unpleasant exchanges with any older or scary kids. Just below the hill that would bring you to the back of Dairy Mart there was a small pile of broken trees covered with an old bed sheet with a couple of broken beach chairs under it. Here big kids used to read bad magazines, drink, and smoke, but now this den of iniquity would be used as the birthplace of the revolution. It really smelled like pee, farts, and skunks, so I didn't want to stay here too long no matter who may be looking for me. I didn't want this to be the smell I would associate with freedom.

I carefully opened the envelope and found a letter written to me by David. I could tell right away it was from him because he was the best in our class at cursive writing. "Nice curves," teachers would tell him, and we would just snicker and roll our eyes. He kept referring to something called "The Broadcast," where what happened at the carnival would be explained and tied in with other, systematic attacks by the Aquatic Apes all over the state of Connecticut and maybe…the world.

"The Broadcast," I kept thinking over and over in my head? This sounded pretty serious because it had a THE in front of the word. Before I could read any more, I heard flippers smacking against the train tracks and coming my way. In a panic, I left the makeshift fort. In my haste to leave, I left David's letter right out in the open. By the time I realized this, I was already running across the street to the Broad Brook Elementary School playground…now my 'old' school.

Knowing there was a squad of these things, I started to feel like Noah Hathaway, Boxey on BATTLESTAR GALACTICA. I used to be so jealous of him running around being chased by Cylons, Ovions, and the aliens of the week, but now…not so much. I hightailed it to the wooded area near the 5th grade wing of the school. I knew I could hide in it for as long as I needed to because no one ever came back here. The path wasn't easy to spot, and everything just grew everywhere and all out of control, so my tracks would be covered. The place was wild with Poison Ivy but for some odd reason it was the only thing I wasn't allergic to. As I hid in the tall, wild grass, I could see the Blueies run right by my position headed for the baseball fields down at the bottom of the hill. I knew it was me they were looking for, so I decided to just wait them out. Going hungry wouldn't be a problem. I had a plastic jar of Raspberry Fluff and a candy bar to dip in it, so I was all set for the long and healthy haul. As I opened the jar of sweet pink goodness, I noticed how the color of the Fluff looked like the Aquatic Apes if it were blue. When the coast was clear an hour or so later, I found a stick and dipped it into the Fluff, drawing an Aquatic Ape on the brick wall. As I stood back and admired my artistic ability I thought ,"Wow, this looks kinda cool." But I realized that the more I admired my handiwork, the more I made myself a target.

Before I bolted away I felt nature's call, went into the sunken-in doorway, and peed. I wasn't big into public urination but man, oh, man, I really had to whiz. Now any guy knows that to achieve perfect letter-making pee ability your pants have to be down just above the knees to execute maximum hip swivel. This was a lot tougher to do in the snow because of the snow pants or snow suits that would bulk you up. Public urination is an art, so I peed my name. Also, Public Urination is against the law.

I decided the best thing for me to do was to just walk down Main Street as if nothing happened, to not only see what was going on around town but to see if the Aquatic Apes were looking for a tall skinny kid with braces and a bowl haircut. As I walked past the businesses that made up Main Street, I looked in the windows from Dairy Mart to the Barn Restaurant to the Opera House. Posters filled the spaces where the carnival flyers were posted a few days before. They were all different, but they all carried the same messages.

AQUATIC APES ARE OUR FRIENDS said one of them. BLUE IS THE COLOR OF

FRIENDSHIP another read with the picture of an Aquatic Ape with two human children in his slimy blue embrace. It was weird seeing these posted in the windows, but even weirder to think where and how did they get these posters made up so fast?

I saw only a few people walking the streets. They all seemed sad and a little lost; completely understandable given the past day's events. After all, this was the end of our world and our way of life because we no longer were in control of our own destinies. It was a horrific sight to see Aquatic Apes walking among us; full families including the little girl ones. It didn't matter what they looked like. They were all taking part in our destruction. As they walked by, I could see people giving them suspicious looks even though everyone was afraid to look them right in the eyes. I remember thinking I was glad to see that we are not smart enough to fall for this charade, seeing these beasts for what they are. Before I could bask in the glory of humanity's intelligence, I saw a sight that I never thought I'd see.

As I neared the post office, a yellow AMC Pacer drove by me with the music blasting the dance-inspired "San Francisco" by the Village People. I watched as the car drove into the post office's small parking lot. The doors swung open on the high performance (and incredibly cool) automobile and two young girls got out. Like good hosts they pulled their seats up to let their backseat passengers out. Like it was happening in slow motion, out of the back seat on both sides of the car came blue, webbed feet. It was two Aquatic Apes, a boy one and a girl one, both looking like teenagers.

The teen-looking Blueies were smiling and laughing as if they knew the driver forever and were lifelong friends. Now this was all really starting to freak me out. I will admit that these Aquatic Apes weren't as threatening as the other, bigger ones walking around town. Sure, the girl one was cute with her shock of blond hair, a pretty bright red bow, and pouty, red lips with long thick lashes, but she was still the enemy. It wasn't lost on me that they all looked naked.

How did they infiltrate everything so *fast?* Much of this would all be revealed tonight during what the letter David entrusted with me, and I subsequently lost, called The Broadcast. This television special would start at 8 PM and be covered on all the networks: ABC, CBS, and NBC! All *three* of them! I hadn't been as excited about a TV event since KISS MEETS THE PHANTOM OF THE PARK, and that was pure awesome!

Before I settled in to watch the broadcast, I cooked myself a nutritious dinner of Chef Boyardee Cheese Ravioli. Despite the metallic taste I got in my mouth eating them because of my braces I still loved them. No meal of mine would be complete without a few Suzi Q's and a lot of Choco-Milk drink to wash it all down. If I was gonna be fighting the good fight and saving the world, I needed to be eating properly and fueled up like Slim Goodbody told us to do. To make it even more official, I ate the ravioli straight out of the can despite the fact that my grandmother always told me I'd get botulism. But of course, I cooked 'em first by putting the can in a pan of boiling water with the label removed. I would eat like this because it was war and that is what soldiers on the front did! They roughed it, and, like it or not, I was now a soldier. Plus, I saw this in an issue of Weird War Tales, in the story "The Day After Doomsday!"

Since I was going to watch this on Channel 8 WTNH out of New Haven, I had to do the usual routine to help with reception. The ABC affiliate was my channel of choice because the stories all seemed like they took place in another world, one so far away and because BATTLESTAR GALACTICA was on ABC! After turning the dial to the number 8, I took the rabbit ear antennae and slide the unit all the way to the back-left corner of the TV. One antenna had to be touching the plant hanging over the set with the other one pointed straight at you. On rainy days we had to hang a soda can pull tab on that end to get an even cleaner signal. We don't know why doing these things worked and it looked kinda silly, but we all did it anyway. You never question science. You just did it. Everyone I knew had their own little tricks to make the picture come in better. I just assumed TV signals coming all the way from far-away New Haven needed plants, cans, and pull tabs to make it all work, maybe because there were a lot of tall buildings and cars in the way.

Appearing on the screen was a big, black number 8 and the words Special Report written underneath it in cool, modern letters. Following a jazzy-influenced musical introduction, the announcer spoke in a cool, deep voice…
"This is an Action News Special Report, coming to you live from the WTNH studios in New Haven, Connecticut. We will return to our regularly scheduled programing following this report. And now, Action News anchor, Pat Sheehan!"

Sitting nervously behind a small desk was the round-faced and re-headed TV news anchor, Pat Sheehan. We all loved this guy probably because he had red hair, and we didn't know a lot of red-haired kids. In front of him was a stack of papers on his desk. Instead of his usual calm and cool demeanor, he seemed a little *off*. This guy would be telling the news standing inside a burning building or shark attack and still be relaxed, so I knew something was wrong. You could see behind his black curtain backdrop that there was some movement and something happening off camera that was drawing his eyes as he began to read off his papers.

"Good evening, Connecticut, this is Pat Sheehan, coming to you live with a fantastic news story right out of BATTLESTAR GALACTICA, appearing Sunday nights on this ABC network. Events have affected many cities and towns in our state, from right here in the city of New Haven to as far north as the quaint and picturesque town of Broad Brook!"

Holy crap, he named our town, feeling a little surge of excitement and for just one second forgetting this was NOT a *good* news report, but still, pride for 06016!

"Over the past week many communities across Connecticut have found

themselves in a unique and…terrifying situation. From out of nowhere, reports have surfaced explaining how we have been attacked, infested, and now subjugated by creatures that resemble those loveable Aquatic Apes we have seen in the ads of funny books that are read by small children or the unintelligent."

Unintelligent? Whaaat you talkin' 'bout, Pat? As he read his report, I noticed him looking off camera at someone, or *something*, that was making him really nervous…and then I saw the unimaginable happen. Without a warning, we witnessed this usually calm newscaster become unhinged. He franticly shuffled the papers on his desk, then did his best to continue…

"But I am here to tell you that these Aquatic Apes…are not a threat to our way of life but are our friends… friends who have returned to rewrite so many of humanity's wrongs. These delightful creatures will amaze us… and become an important part of our society. Many of these Aquatic Apes have already been reunited with the human hosts that raised them until someone in their home decided to end their lives by flushing them down the toilet, or pouring them down a cold, dark, and lonely sink. Those people have been or WILL be dealt with under the Aquatic Apes holy book, the Law of the Living Plasma."

The screen made a quick cut to a couple of kids, all wearing sunglasses and about my age who were standing in front of a brick building with the beach directly behind them.

"We were here at the Paperback Trader, me and Al and Danny," said Mitchell Hallock of New Haven as his name appeared on the bottom of the screen. "We were getting comic books and stuff when all of a sudden this Aquatic Ape-looking thing took Al away. It freaked us out, man!" Mitchell then began to point toward the direction they exited. "When they took Dave away, he was kicking and screaming, but we were too scared to do anything about it." Scared or not, that Mitch dude was just on TV…lucky, but yes, sad for his loss.

Then the cut ended and returned back to the Channel 8 studios.

I moved even closer at the TV. As Pat held his script, I noticed something very odd. While Sheehan read the news, I saw the back of the papers had words written on them only in view of the camera and the viewing audience. Since the picture wasn't crystal clear like if I was watching Channel 3 out of Hartford, I had to play with the antennae a bit until I could read what was written in dark red letters. When I saw the words, my blood chilled!

THEY ARE THE ENEMY!

Wowza…this hit me as hard as "we have traced the call and it is coming from inside the house," from that scary movie I wasn't allowed to see! Now it was obvious…these Aquatic Ape things were up to no good and now Pat Sheehan was telling us this. If you can't trust Pat Sheehan, who can you trust? Someone must have seen the messages that Pat was sending to the viewers, because all of a sudden two rather large Aquatic Apes aggressively grabbed him and forced him away from his desk, kicking and screaming, and I think swearing, too. With their high-pitched bubbly voices, I could hear them yelling at him as they began to hit him with their flippery hands like flapping blue dervishes! Then without any warning the screen was filled with the color test pattern and that high-pitched signal boooooooohhhhhhhhhhhh tone. Before this moment, I only saw and heard it to represent the end of the broadcast day, but now that meant the end of humanity and life as we knew it.

Then as fast as it left, the picture came back with pops and crackles and now we saw a tall man seated at the desk looking very worried. You could see that the desk had blood on it and for some reason a man's dress shoe with maybe with a foot still in it. I really couldn't tell from my vantage point. On this young man's left and right stood two Aquatic Apes, smiling that creepy little smile they always have on their faces. His eyes were wide open and his mouth looked like it was trying to formulate words, but nothing seemed to be coming out. Then the Aquatic Ape on his left grabbed his shoulder and nudged him, urging him to read a new clean set of papers that were placed in front of him, and he began to read. He spoke without any emotion, but a slight Pennsylvanian accent and never looked up from the papers. Despite the fact that he was sitting sixty miles away from me and I could only see him from my Curtis Mathes TV screen, I could sense much fear.

"Good evening, everyone. My name is Steve Stevens and I'm here to tell you all that the Aquatic Apes are our friends and whatever has been negatively said or implied is a lie. They have only returned to claim that which belongs to them. They are sorry that they had to flush some of the humans who got in their way, but that is how Aquatic Apes live and they are justified in their actions. If necessary, they will do it again and again. What has happened in your state will play itself out over the next six to eight weeks all across the country, and the world… wherever Aquatic Apes were sold…and wronged!"

Tears began to swell up in his eyes as he flipped to the next paper. He continued, almost forcing himself to say words he didn't agree with, but he had to read. If this Steve Stevens guy resisted, he may be flushed!

"The Aquatic Apes were a peaceful, almost docile race, swimming in their little bowls performing tricks until the time of the great flushing! As their societies were flushed and purged, they settled into the sewage treatment plants, sewers, rivers, and septic systems of Anytown USA. Many of those who fought to survive were purged with the power of the green fluorspar. Here they waited, and waited, until they could grow to fruition and begin to take back what was rightfully theirs. Coming up after this commercial break we will hear from Professor Herman von Braun, coming to you live from Memphis, Tennessee!"

Memphis? Wait…*what?* The story from GRIT and that guy Jeff? Now this was all beginning to make a lot more sense. But suddenly I got distracted by some commercials. No, I wasn't going to knock the battery off of Robert Conrad's shoulder, yes, I loved McDonald's, and I never thought of myself as being a Pepper, but I loved commercials. It was nice to see that the Aquatic Apes invasion had sponsorship. With everything happening around me, I was starting to see that I was easily distracted by shiny rocks and cool TV commercials. I couldn't do math to save my life, but I could recite every commercial for almost any product: soap, detergent, fast foods, soda. No matter what it was, I knew it. Six times six? That may take some time. Cuckoo-For-Cocoa-Puffs? That meant something.

When Steve Stevens the reporter came back on set, he looked a little worse for wear, like he was on the losing end of a dodgeball game with 8th Graders. Now, there was an Aquatic Ape, a big, angry, and mean-looking one, standing directly behind him with his webbed flippers all over his shoulders, like he was reminding him who was in charge. It was obvious by this guy's appearance that he also had taken issue with what he was being told to report but he didn't appear to suffer the same brutal fate as poor Pat Sheehan did. What we would now be told from this moment on would set the tone for this entire event. There would be no more games and no more beating around the bush. It was truth time, Aquatic Ape style.

"Welcome back to this special report coming to you live from the WTNH-TV studios in New Haven, CT. If you are just joining us, Aquatic Apes have made their presence known in several cities and towns in the Nutmeg State as well as points all over the world. This is not a hoax or part of any game. This is the first Will and Testament of the Aquatic Apes. Words like that made this darker and certainly a more desperate situation. They are not here to make friends or be a part of our society. They are here to subjugate us, and, if necessary, to destroy us if need be. Big Gulp! For almost thirty years, humans have bought Aquatic Apes, hatched families, and helped create their lives. Then, once they got bored or angry that they didn't look like they did in the comic book ads, their human hosts dumped them into sinks and toilet, killing millions. This ends now!"

Then, without any warning at all, the reporter was forcefully removed from his chair and a much larger and less happy-looking Aquatic Ape sat down in the chair and faced the camera. The evil and anger in his eyes burned right into my soul, all the way from New Haven. He wasn't as blue as the others, but almost purple and bruised, looking like he had been burned with cuts and scrapes all over his face. Unlike the other Blueies, he wore a jacket, a bright red American Revolution style coat complete with wide white lapels, piping, and gold-laced trim down the front. There were even several medals pinned to it, and I'm not sure I wanted to know what he got them for. Where would an Aquatic Ape even *get* a coat? I must say, despite the fact that he was looking to exterminate us, he looked *very* cool. Then I thought once again that 204 Revolutionary War Soldiers have come back to bite me!

"All hail Aquatic Apes!! Flush one and six more will take its place!"

Okay, this thing had my full attention. His voice had that high-pitched Bee Gees bubble thing going on, but not as funny. This one meant business.

"My name is Flippy Pete and I'm in charge of the Aquatic Ape forces in your state. Many years ago, in this very city, the seeds to our uprising were planted! At one time our mighty creator developed us as soldiers, but in a time of peace we became an instrument for fun. We became amusement for little children everywhere, especially those who lived in small apartments that couldn't have a pet like a cat or a dog! Our creator created life from plain water, eggs, and living plasma! We would delight and amaze our human hosts and do tricks and enjoy them using the magnifying orbs in our homes, watching us in amazement, until we didn't grow anymore, and we resembled simple Brine Shrimp! That is where your ignorance became your downfall. As depicted by the sacred drawings of Joe, it would have taken us one full year to begin to develop into the magnificence you see before you. It was your impatience and cruelty that you now paying for."

Ummmmmm, Flippy Pete? Okay, so maybe we were wrong to jump the gun and just flush 'em down a toilet, but to be honest and in our defense, we didn't know they would get big and angry. By now this obviously excitable and bossy Aquatic Ape had his own agenda.

"Once I was in a tank with my family and friends, enjoying everything the creator gave us until one day a bright blue eye looked at us through the magnifying orb. This eye was not like the normal brown one that would feed us, love us, and watch over us. This blue eye looked down on us, shook our home when he was alone with us, and then dropped an object in the water that secreted a fiery acid that not only turned our home brown, but burned all of us…killing all but me!"

You could see the anger take him over, and, hearing that story, who could blame him? He had become pure hate because of something someone did to him.

"I was able to survive by sheer will, divine intervention, and the sizzled carcasses of my family. When their bodies rose to the top, I floated on them until a few days later we were poured into a pit outside. There, we were all but forgotten. But I didn't forget! Since we will never know the owner of the blue-eyed devil who destroyed us, we will make it our mission to destroy them all, every blue eye! This is where our war began, and this will be where our war will end. There will be blood in the streets in the town of New Haven!"

UH-OH! This had now turned into something real serious, and I don't think this problem will just go away in time. These things seem to not only have a reason to wipe us out, but they certainly have the numbers and the will to do it. I mean, there were millions of them sold worldwide from 1957 to today and it seems that their end didn't come from a simple flushing.

Then there were some crackles and pops coming from the TV like the old movies we saw in school from a film projector. Suddenly a ghostly image appeared on the screen. The out-of-focus picture soon cleared up and I saw on the screen an older man. He was a scientific-looking guy who was a little creepy, complete with a lab coat and goggles around his neck, and, when he spoke, he had a German accent. "Of course, he did," I commented to myself.

"Gootevenink, Amerika! My name is Professor Herman von Braunn and I come to you with visions of a new world, MY WORLD!"

OK, so far that doesn't sound too threatening.

"In 1942 back home in my native Germany, I vas one of the greatest scientifik minds the Third Reich had ever seen. At that time our armies ver fighting many aggressors in very distinct climates: the snow and cold of Russia, the sun and sands of Africa, und der general climates of Europe. As we ver fighting all over the vorld we knew that we needed more soldiers to fill der ranks and plan our attacks on Amerika! As ve vorked on this, ve also needed a superior soldier; one who could be transported easily and be able to grow and work in any climates. My first attempts were unsuccessful until I discovered Cryptobiosis, a process vitch is an ametabolic state of life entered by an organism in response to adverse environmental conditions like freezing or being oxygen deprived!"

What now, doc?

"In the cryptobiotic state, all metabolic processes stop, preventing reproduction, development, and repair."

OK doc… blah, blah, blah…you're losing me here with all this science speak!

"In other vords, I can put life into a packet; just add water and then… instant life anyvhere I vant it! These were going to be the new soldiers, heroes, and saviors of the Fatherland, but by the time I could make them grow beyond their small, shrimplike stage the var was sadly over and ve had lost. We ver cheated of our destiny and our divine right to rule the vorld had passed…or so ve thought! Following the war, I escaped to the United States, the country I hold responsible for the death of the Third Reich, to unleash my soldiers…my Fourth Reich! It took me almost ten more years to perfect my soldiers and now my children are everyvhere! I have almost taken over the entire state of Connecticut and after I achieve victory there, I will move my troops into Massachusetts, then I will take over that little state in between them, and then the world. Victory will be ours! Heil…ME!"

Then came the requisite maniacal laugh with fist clenched which went on for a few long uncomfortable minutes. As the screen went blank for a few seconds I wondered…was this the end times? What was I supposed to do now? I started to hyperventilate and get a little panicky. Before I started to go into complete meltdown mode about my predicament, the MUPPET SHOW came on. It's amazing how a chorus line of Muppets, special guest star Elton John, and a bunch of Muppet crocodiles can make a little guy feel okay. The magic of television!

"It's time to put on makeup, it's time to light the lights, it's time to get thing started on the Muppet Show tonight…" Ahhhh, the Muppets! Amazing what a hand and some fabric can do to make a kid feel good.

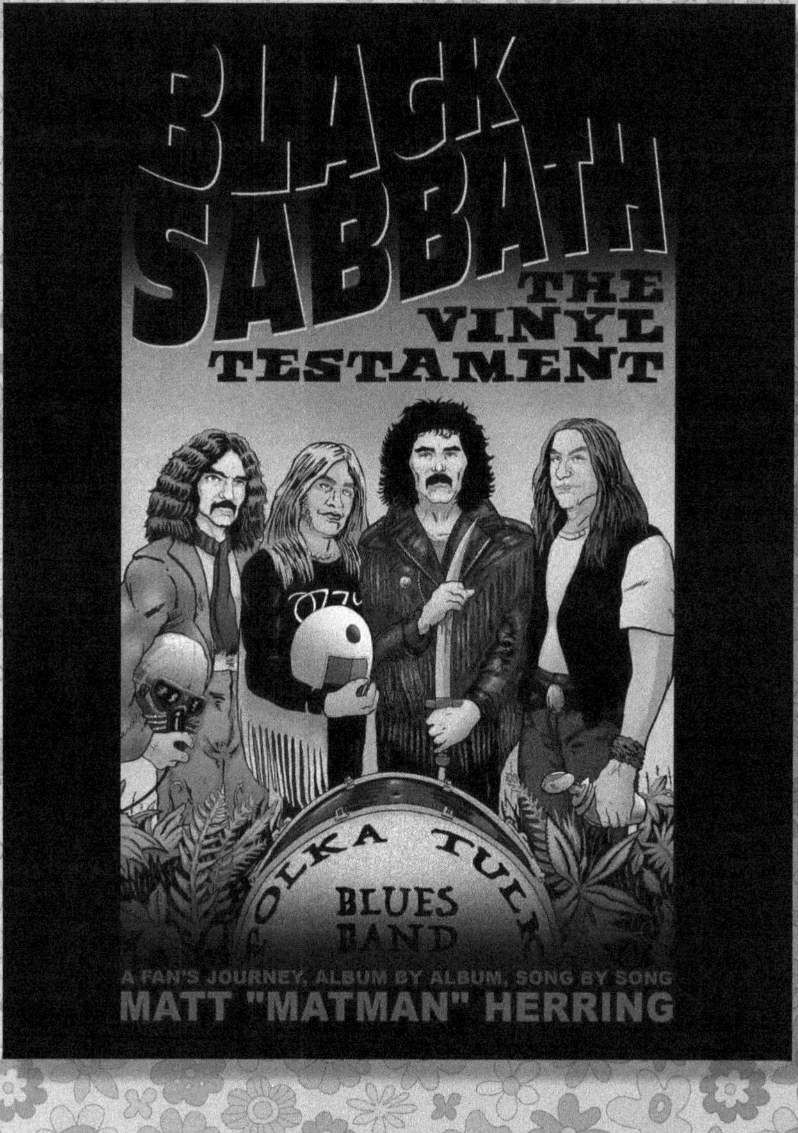

hair
teeth
Sun-in
THE LOOK YOU WANT—
WHEN YOU WANT IT!
X-Ray Spex
See bones thru skin
See thru clothing
AMAZING
X-RAY VISION
Guaranteed!
THE FAMOUS Blushingly FUNNY ILLUSION
X-RAY VISION
204 REVOLUTIONARY WAR SOLDIERS
ONLY $1.98

CHAPTER FIVE
"Trying to _Get the Feeling_ Again"

The roundup or the collecting of humans has now begun!

We all tried to just go on with our lives like nothing was going on but we couldn't do it for the obvious reasons because something was.

Everywhere you looked there were Aquatic Apes and that brought on a lot of stress for everyone. You couldn't miss their big, tall, stupid, blue bodies and those dumb smiles on their faces. Swing sets and slides…Aquatic Apes! Tennis court… Aquatic Apes! Jungle gym…Aquatic Apes! The only place they weren't ever hanging out was in the swimming pool, probably because of all the chlorine and other crazy chemical concoctions my dad used to pour in there. It was strange to see someone else roll out the big blue barrel of chemicals to the pool because my family was now in hiding, but hey…a man, or boy, still has to swim. In charge of chemical distribution now was Mark, an older guy of 23 years old. He was a good looking Italian dude complete with Italian horn chain and a red Trans Am. It wasn't much of a surprise that my sister, and probably everyone's sister, had a crush on him. From this moment on he was now the chemical man! He looked over at me and we did the "what's up" head nod to each other, but without my blue-eyed friends like Kerry, Kirk, and Jason, pool life wasn't quite the same. I didn't know what was happening to them or to anyone else the Aquatic Apes considered blue-eyed devils, but I was thankful for having brown eyes.

As I swam around the pool in my own little world, I was oblivious to the fact that someone slipped a note into my rolled-up HAPPY DAYS Fonzie towel. When I was all done swimming, I got out of the water, my skin dried out and eyes burning from the overdose of chlorine. I picked up my towel and saw the note fall out. Before I picked it up, I looked around to see if anyone was watching me and to make sure this wasn't a trap. Was anyone watching me suspiciously, or at all? After seeing Blueies get out of a car yesterday, I realized I couldn't trust anyone anymore. I subtly picked up the note, slid it into my towel, and walked away with my eyes in the air and whistling…or as I like to call it, just being slick.

In the comfort of my own super-cool room, I opened the slightly damp note and read it. Before I got to that point, I heard the siren song of the ice cream truck. Something about the ding-dong cart that makes everything seem at least not too bad. I had to see my man Tyler and get my usual fix, a Frightful Frank Hoodwink for now and a Cannonball complete with a wooden spoon for later. Wrapped in white paper, the wooden spoon was as important as the ice cream or sherbet you would scoop it with. When I was done using it, I would suck on it until it got splintery and then I would try to crack it with my canine teeth. No wonder I needed braces. I think someone famous once said you can't save the world without ice cream, and that someone was me. After my treat, I went back upstairs and opened the letter. As I read it, I could hear the voice of George C. Scott as

General George Patton reading it in my head.

   Dear Matt! As you can see from everything going on, this has become some pretty serious business! These blue demons mean to end humanity under their slimy webbed feet unless we fight back! As you help to organize the resistance, I will be able to help you only from a distance because I am a very wanted man! If I was ever caught, I would be stripped of my skin, boiled alive by the Aquatic Apes, and fed to their young, so I must remain in the shadows. I have agents everywhere and you have already met one of them, Mr. Pincus. I have been told by the powers in control at the Revolution that you are someone we can trust and put our faith into. Make no mistake, Matt, this is a war, a war for the survival of the human race. You will be asked to do things you never thought you would ever be asked to do and put yourself in situations that only the fighting soldier has ever faced. You must have faith that your playtime and training, recreating the great battles of the American Revolution with your 204 Revolutionary War Soldiers, has given you what it will take to make a difference. We will be in touch!

   Damn, not the Revolutionary War soldiers again!!! That red and blue playset will be my *downfall!*

   I could feel my emotions being pulled in so many different directions, like a Mego Stretch Armstrong or its green cousin, the Stretch Hulk. With the weight of the free world on my shoulders, I decided to take a walk to Pigeon's Pharmacy to get more comic books and some lunch at the food counter, and also think about what my next plan was. I realized I needed a disguise, something to alter my appearance in case they were looking for me, but nothing too drastic. I remember seeing a commercial on TV for a spray-on product called Sun-In, which would make my brown hair blonde, naturally, with the help of the sun. As the commercial said, it was available at most fine drug stores. Perfect. Before I left. I went into my fake moustache kit to find a look that would help me change it up a bit. A few years back I had sent a few bucks to the Honor House in New York for a collection of sideburns, moustaches, and something called a Van Dyke that would cover my chin. This would have been a foolproof disguise except I filled out the order coupon wrong and got all-natural red hair, which is not a match for my all-natural brown hair, but I'd have to somehow make it work.

   I sat at the food counter waiting for my well-done cheeseburger, fries, and Coke with a little bit of ice. I noticed others sitting around enjoying their food, including a group of Aquatic Apes sitting with humans in the corner booth, the smoking section. Filling the airwaves was "Shadow Dancing" by Andy Gibb, floating on top of the comforting conversations and subtle noises associated with a food counter. My ten-year-old ears could also hear the blip-blip-blip of someone's handheld Coleco Electronic Quarterback. I needed to find that person and play a game or ten. There were also a few Aquatic Apes sitting at the counter five stools down, and, in my paranoia, and itchy Van Dyke, I thought they were looking directly at me. I tried to look away and not make eye contact with them, but I was so curious to see what they were eating. I risked a snoopy peak and saw it was…salad. How tough could they be eating lettuce? I would hate to think what they would be like if they were meat eaters.

"Crazy how these things just walk around town like they have always been here," said a guy sitting right next to me wearing the same Van Dyke disguise as I was only with a better color match. "Disgusting blue creatures! It's like they own the place!" I was almost afraid to agree with him since I was becoming a little paranoid and didn't know who to trust anymore, fake moustache or not.

In the past few days, I had seen Aquatic Apes driving around in cars with humans. I had seen them in the fields playing kickball with human kids, so I knew they had started to infiltrate our society and way of life pretty quickly. To be honest, if I'm captain of a kickball team choosing sides, I'm gonna pick one of these webbed-footed goons. They can kick the ball a ton and probably could hit the stage in the elementary school gymnasium. That was every boy's dream before they went on to Middle School; hit the stage with a kickball in the air with no bouncies. If you didn't hit the stage before you moved on, it could prove to be a lifetime of regret.

As I waited for my food to arrive, I saw a fellow comic book enthusiast, Daryl, and his daughter, Kayley, working their way through their lunches. I waved to Daryl, who gave me a half-hearted wave back wondering why there was a ten-year-old kid with facial hair getting his attention...hair that wasn't there yesterday.

"Matt?" he asked inquisitively, "What's up with the disguise?" I slid into the booth with that cool, crushing leather sound. As I sat down, I could see it was Kayley playing the football game. BLIP-BLIP-BLIP!

"I'm hiding from the Aquatic Apes," I told him. "I think I'm wanted." Daryl looked incredibly concerned, probably because I was now putting him and his daughter in grave danger.

"I like Aquatic Apes," she told us, drawing more Apes on her napkin when she wasn't playing the game. "They are just so cool." Trying not to scare his daughter, Daryl leaned toward me and used the latest issue of PULP GALLERY MAGAZINE to hide our conversation.

"You got to get out of here, now," he warned me! "Yesterday I saw them rounding up people and herding them into that crazy castle thing at the carnival ground." He looked concerned for me. "If those things are after you, then you better run away…fast!"

As I started to get up, Kayley handed me a picture that had an Aquatic Ape and a human, holding hands with the word FRIEND on top of it. I took it and just smiled, not wanting to frighten her with a bad reaction. Kayley looked at them as friends with the innocence only a child could. I didn't want to scare her with the truth, so I just got up and left.

I grabbed my brown bag containing my plain cheeseburger and soda, paid for my STARLOG and CREEPY magazines and a couple bottles of Sun-In and made my way outside. I walked past a few Aquatic Apes standing by the clothing donation drop-off out in front by the fence and started to get a little nervous. Were these a few of the Blueies that chased me? I couldn't tell because they all look the same to me. I did notice these two whispering and staring me down as I walked past them. They mumbled to each other and let me pass, but I admit it got me a little worried. As I crossed the bridge facing the Broad Brook Opera House, I could see a few more of them looking at a blown-up photograph. Oh man, was it *me?*

Do they know about the *notes?* Do they know about me drawing an Aquatic Ape on the school wall and then *peeing* on it? I pretended to drop something, and, as slick as I could be, got a bit closer to see the picture and was shocked to see what it was. "OH NO," I said out loud and not in my head like I thought. Apparently, my startled expression drew the attention of the two Blueies. In the picture…in full glossy black and white…there it was! My Marshmallow FLUFF Aquatic Apes drawing I did on the wall! The worst part of it was to the lower far left. You could see a little dude from the back…*peeing!* I didn't know what my own butt looked like, but I knew who those cheeks belonged to me!

Not wanting them to recognize the back of my head, I began walking by them backwards. I walked across the bridge that way, almost tripping into traffic a few times, and kept myself incognito. The Aquatic Apes seemed a little suspicious and slightly amused at my deception, but they didn't move.

When I knew I was in the clear, I turned around and hightailed it towards the old semi-abandoned mill, or, as we knew it, the place where kids would go to do bad things. At this moment, I felt it was time to hide for my own safety. I made my way through the dark labyrinth of halls, empty rooms, and rotted floorboards. I stumbled, almost tripping over a box that just was lying in the middle of the hallway. From where it was placed it appeared that I was meant to find it. I dragged the box toward the back of the mill into a well-lit area to see what was inside. Sure, it could have been a bomb or a dismembered body, but it also could have been OFFICIAL DETECTIVE magazines, so you can see where my brain was… or wasn't. I opened the box and put my hand straight into the pile of foam peanuts. I dug my hands in deep and reached around until I found something inside. A box? A box inside a box? This could be interesting. As I brought the box to the surface of the sea of green foam, I was able to finally read what it said on the box.

"X-Ray Specs," I read aloud, "See through skin and clothing?"

Of all the things I *NEVER* ordered or even cared about, it was X-Ray Specs. The idea always seemed kinda dumb to me and I was pretty sure they didn't work. When I got accidentally hit in the face with a baseball bat at the end of the school year, I had to have a big machine take the pictures to see if anything in my face was broken, and, thankfully, nothing was. If these glasses really worked, there would have been a bunch of people wearing those at Rockville Hospital looking for broken face bones.

"Ummm, with my X-Ray Specs I see no breaks," Doctor Lenhert would tell me. "Hmmmmmm," Doctor Giarrusso would say, cleaning the lenses off on his tie. "Ahhhh yup, I don't see any breaks." I opened up the box, pulled out a pair, and placed them on my face. I put my hand out, fanning my fingers and waving them in front of my eyes. What I saw shocked and slightly amazed me! It almost looked like I could see the bones in my *hand!* Maybe I *misjudged* them?

Thinking these things on my face might actually help me get home without drawing too much suspicion, I walked back out into the light of day with the box tucked under my arm. When I came out of the building onto the sidewalk there were a group of Aquatic Apes hanging out with a small group of people, including my friends Missy, Gary, and his freaky weird little sister whose name I don't even remember.

"Hey, Matt," yelled Missy. "You have to meet our new friends. They are so nice and funny!"

Not wanting to look like I was hiding anything, I walked up to the group and said hi. When I looked at the Aquatic Apes with the X-Ray Specs on, I saw that those toothy smiles and smiling eyes that were constantly on their faces were no longer there. What I saw was scary-looking glowing eyes, mouths full of nasty razor teeth, and a forked tongue. They kind of looked like the way I pictured the Devil looking like, minus his pitchfork. Looking at my friends, they were nothing but a little blurry. Missy, Garry, and his creepy sister whose name I don't remember all looked the same. When I removed the glasses, the Aquatic Apes looked like we have been seeing them. I quickly put them back on and once again I saw the crazy faces, but I also noticed something very interesting. Their blue bodies were no longer solid, but transparent, like a freaked-out Slim Goodbody! "Yuk," I said to myself. Another weird thing I noticed, among all the other junk, was a bright red ball floating inside their bodies, just bouncing around their insides, like that stuff inside a lava lamp. Again, with the glasses off, I didn't see anything like that.

Wait a stinking minute!!!

Maybe these glasses show the wearer what these things really looked like? I was concerned that people would start to fall in love with these cute and loveable-looking things, and then, with our defenses down, they could move in and kill us while we slept. Or they could just take us out right out in the open since they seemed to be in charge of everything now? As I held the box tighter, I started to walk away faster than normal. As I crossed the street near the waterfall, Missy came running toward me, took my arm, and forced me to walk away even faster from the group. "Did she know something," I thought?

"Matt, I need to tell you something kinda weird," Missy said, pulling me down closer to her to bridge our height difference. Giggling a bit, she said to me, "I think one of the Aquatic Apes has a crush on me." She looked back at them all standing there looking dumb, especially Gary's googly sister, "And I'm not sure which one." Then she ran back to the group.

It was mind-boggling how, in the course of a few weeks, life as we knew it was over. As I walked down Depot Street past the pond on my left, I started to feel a little sad for the first time since all this happened. Would we ever get to skate on the pond again? Would I ever see my *family* again? The town had changed so much. I used to see Crazy Tommy sitting on the steps of Steve's Spirit Shoppe teaching the kids swear words as they walked by. Covering the windows would be signs and posters for things like Schlitz, Pabst Blue Ribbon, and something called Boones Farm Wine. Now those pictures were covered up by posters showing the Aquatic Apes as our friends, all happy holding beer, and smoking cigarettes. Where did they get these made up so quickly? It reminded me of the cool-looking propaganda art I saw in books about World War Two, but not as cool because this was affecting me. A bit up the street the windows of the local Kelly-Fradet Lumber were covered in this Bluey propaganda art, instead of the usual signs reading "Hammers 6/$3.00" or "We Have Toilets!" I clutched my fists to show my anger to no one in particular. Now I had a box of X-Ray Specks to show that truth to everyone! As I turned toward my townhouse, I kept thinking that I needed to organize all my friends and even some of the bigger, older, mean kids. How could I bring them all together?

"Hey Matt," said my pal, Robert, walking with his little brother, Michael. "See you at the STAR WARS club meeting tonight?" I nodded yes, still trying to find a way to secretly organize my friends without creating suspicion. Further up the street, Jack and Shawn were running around the little fenced-in area by my house trying to catch snakes. They both asked if we were still going to have our meeting that night considering what was going on and I yelled, "YES!" Nothing, not even an Aquatic Apes invasion with friends and family being taken away, could stop us in our discovery of more secrets about the greatest space fantasy film of all time! We were all getting STAR WARS crazier considering STAR WARS II was coming out the following May. Wait a minute…I thought. I could use the meeting that night to discuss how we could fight back…following, of course, our discussion of STAR WARS.

As I walked into my empty house, I could hear a splash and happy screams! Apparently, Jack and/or Shawn, they were twins so I couldn't ever tell which was which, fell into the pond chasing a snake that they would for some reason name Scott.

From the Sea

Lyrics and Music By Brendan Clark
©Mysticism and Mischief Music (BMI)

New England Breeze, carefree day, feels of summertime
Sunshine illuminates the sky, A wondrous state of mind
Still the joy that surrounds the carnival atmosphere
Something lurks, sinister, With a sense of dread and fear

A sight I saw, to my shock, that I could not believe
Attacking this New England town, Oh Monkeys from the Sea
Carnage, havoc and dismay, all we can do is run
Oh futile and not long ago Seems our summertime fun

From the Sea, cloaked in revelry
Desperately we run for our lives
Fear in the air, Monkeys everywhere
Destruction, despair, this could be our demise

From the Sea, cloaked in revelry
Desperately we run for our lives
Fear in the air, Monkeys everywhere
Destruction, despair, this could be our demise

Revulsed at the fairground, thought struck as Broad Brook is being tore down
Aquatic Apes abound that run a-muck
But the pages I read inspire thoughts to construct

We hatch a plan to fight back with naive confidence
By no other means could we find, could come to our defense
Nothing stops a youthful will with defiance in their soul
Face the challenge spit in their eye, refused to be controlled

From the Sea, cloaked in revelry
Desperately we run for our lives
Fear in the air, Monkeys everywhere
Destruction, despair, this could be our demise

From the Sea
From the Sea
From the Sea
From the Sea

HAIR
X-RAY VISION
TEETH
SPLINTER OF THE MINDS EYE
Alan Dean Foster
TRANSPARENT BLUE
BIG TOO GRIN
GLOWING EYE
WEBBED FEET
WACKY 102FM

CHAPTER SIX
"Sweet Life"

Like clockwork, everyone arrived at my house for our weekly meeting of the Friends of the Jedi, the unofficial STAR WARS Fan Club of Broad Brook, CT 06016, that we had started a few months back. Each week, we would meet up at a different place, and if the weather was good, we would even hold our meetings outside under the stars. For our super-special 11th meeting, it was the cool basement at 5-F Townhouse Road, complete with beanbag chairs and a freezer full of Freeze Pops to propel our discussions. Now I considered myself to be the biggest STAR WARS fan of all, but it was Leo who even I was a little in awe of. Despite the fact that I had all the figures, vehicles, comic books, and cards, it was Leo who had the coveted STAR WARS EARLY BIRD CERTIFICATE. This came out prior to the figures being made and available, sort of an IOU from Kenner Toys that you will get them, this is what they look like, we just haven't made them yet. To us, this made him the first true fan...and he loved comic books, too, so that wa a plus as well as him being a real con man!

Despite the world seemingly falling apart around us, we had our usual 15 club members there to discuss the important issues of the day, STAR WARS! No Aquatic Apes invasion was ever gonna keep us from getting together. As the host I was in charge of leading the meeting and bringing up discussion question. for us to talk about in detail. Our first order of business was to discuss the recent article in DYNAMITE magazine about how STAR WARS was now considered the fourth movie in the series, part of a proposed trilogy of trilogies that would be made out of order. This made no sense to any of us, but we tried to discuss it as best we could. We would also begin our countdown to STAR WARS II that was now less than a year away!

"Darth Vader got so beat up by Ben Kenobi for killing Luke's dad that he now ha to wear all that black armor to help him breathe," interjected Jason, one of our younger members.

"He fought Obi-Wan and fell into a lava pit and caught on fire," said Scott, a member who traveled from Warehouse Point added to the discussion.

As the conversations reached their natural conclusions, I had to bring up the most controversial STAR WARS subject that even seemed to be pulling our own group apart...was SPLINTER OF THE MIND'S EYE going to be the next STAR WARS movie? Despite my love of the book, I didn't think it would be the next film because Chewie and Han weren't in it and Darth Vader got his arm chopped off but try changing the minds of Eddie and Jeff who would argue it was, until they started to go all ROCKY on everyone and punch us into submission. When this would start to happen, we immediately changed our focus to STAR WARS cards and who needed what to distract everyone from the arguing.

As the popsicles were finished and cards and stickers were all traded, I decided now would be a good time to bring up the reality of the situation outside in the real world.

"New business," I declared as I pulled out the box I found in the old mill and handed a pair of X-Ray Specs to everyone. "Everyone grab a pair and put 'em on."

"What are these?" Oz asked. "They aren't even STAR WARS-related!"

I told everyone to sit for a minute as I pulled out some notes to go over with my crew. "We all know that weeks ago Aquatic Apes came out of nowhere and destroyed the carnival, took away some people, and are now walking around town bossing us around." Most of the kids seemed pretty angry at them but one of us, Edgar, seemed a little confused by what I just said. "I have gotten letters from someone who I have never met, who was telling me about this before it even happened." I lifted up the letters to show them but didn't let anyone touch or read them.

"They are all over the place," Perry yelled, who saw his dad taken away by the Aquatic Apes two days ago. "I hate them all!" We all did. I was really sad for Perry. I know how I would feel if my dad was taken away.

"I was talking to an Aquatic Ape yesterday at the post office," Edgar told us, "and I thought he was real cool", Edgar told us. "They are nice, and I just want to be friends, so I invited him to the meeting."

"What?" I yelled with full drama and excitement. almost hearing the old radio show music played to describe terror. "Coming *here?*" I started to panic. My heart began to pound like it did when I almost drowned last year, because of Edgar's brother. "Here?" I yelled, getting all excited and not in a good way, *"HERE?!"* My sudden outburst made Peter and Danny start to cry and yell how they wanted to go home…which was right next door. I grabbed my notes, a green Popsicle, and the box of X-Ray Specs and started to run upstairs with everyone following me up the loud, shaky cellar steps. As I hit the top of the stairs, I could hear something moving on my front porch. I quietly moved closer to the door and opened the little lever covering the peephole on the front door. Through the slot I saw twelve of those antennae things on the other side of my front door. I motioned to everyone to run out the back door into the woods towards the hill behind G Townhouse. Since it was getting a little dark out, half the kids didn't want to go because the woods could be a scary place and I agreed, but a front step full of Aquatic Apes was a lot scarier to me.

There was a well-trampled path that led from the woods behind my house to a large hill near the Scantic River. This is where we would play war all day long, but, as I had to remind myself, we weren't just playing war anymore. As we tore off into the woods, I could still hear Eddie and Jeff arguing about SPLINTER OF THE MINDS EYE.

Running down the path before we got to the hill was a bit tricky to navigate in the daytime let alone in the dark. As you get to the bottom of this narrow path there is a tree smack dab in the middle of it that you need to quickly move to the left and duck, so you don't whack yourself in the face with this huge branch. If you walk it, you can do this okay, but we never walked. We were always running. Past the tree you come up the hill and just as soon as you get to the top there is a huge drop straight down about 100 or so feet into the river. We always thought about how cool it would be to slide or sled down toward the river, but there were rocks, roots, and downed trees all the way down that created the agony of defeat threat. Last winter, while scaling the other side, Kirk and Russell joined me trying to climb up the hill. Then we all met up at the bottom in a bruised and dirty heap with Russell sliding all the way into the water.

Once we got to the top, we carefully walked down the left side into a little covered area where we could catch our breath and hide pretty undetected. In the past year, a large crater covered by a fallen tree was our sacred spot when avoiding bullies, like Roscoe or Richie, who wandered into the neighborhood looking to pick on us.

I took a head count and saw that only eight of us, including me, made it to the safe zone. As we all sat there bewildered, a little disoriented, and somewhat out of breath, I decided to tell the guys all about the glasses.

"I found these at the mill," I told the group, adding to my coolness because I went into the mill. "When you put them on they show you what the Aquatic Apes really look like." Everyone tried on a pair and looked at each other and then at their hands, all giggling. Mark was the first to speak up.

"These are junk like those stupid bats I ordered last year," he yelled. "They didn't climb up the window or make noise or scare anyone...and I was out a *buck!*"

Then *everyone* started yelling about all the comic ads they got ripped off from, forgetting we were now being hunted! Danny's 100 Dolls (we didn't ask why he ordered them), Ronald's Super Siren for his bike that broke within a week of him putting it on his handlebars and almost getting him run over. And we never heard the end of Derek's Camping Survival kit story. "The stupid tent was made out of Reynolds Wrap," he said, "and the PA horn didn't work! I almost died out there!" It became an eight-way loud conversation that I'm sure people could hear all the way to China, where most of this stuff was made.

Shell Shock was settling in and I needed to get order restored!

"Okay, guys, listen up! I know we have all been the victims of some bad scams and comic book ads that didn't deliver what they promised, like my free Boba Fet but I will not let any of you speak badly about ALL comic book ads! We all have seen the benefits of some cool stuff, too." I looked around at the group, all still wearing the glasses, and pointed at Mac. "*Mac,* you were always getting sand kicked in your face at the Reservoir by big kids until you sent away for that Tony

Atlas thing." He smiled and nodded in agreement, giving me the thumbs-up. "*Now* look at you! You're sharing a blanket with 7th Grade girls and kicking chairs all over your room." He was starting to turn red from embarrassment. Although we were all starting to like girls, none of us were ready to admit it yet.

"Now Michael plays a mean guitar and writes his own songs because of a comic book ad, right?" Michael, who now seemed so much cooler than the rest of us because of the guitar, just smiled. "And how about *you*, Rick?" I motioned to Rick, sitting in the corner looking over the top of the hole like a true soldier at the front. "Rick's dad trusted him with a Daisy BB Rifle like hockey legend Bobby Hull did with his sons. And what did *Rick* do? He shot out all the windows at the abandoned train depot and got in trouble with the police…but his dad never found out, so the trust is still there!" Rick gave me the thumbs-up, beaming with lawbreaking pride.

'Who among us doesn't enjoy the great foods that Hostess brings us? Fruit Pies, Suzy–Q's, and Twinkies not only are good for us, but they help superheroes stop real bank robbers and invading space aliens. *Remember that* the next time the world turns upside down and a delicious Hostess Fruit Pie is the only thing standing between you and certain doom!" Then I wondered if a fruit pie could ever save us but decided to just let it go. With pride I beamed, thinking I proved that not all comic book ads are junk. "Except Lemon Fruit Pies," yelled Justin, "those things are nasty!" We all agreed. *(Lemon Fruit Pies **are** awesome. -EDITOR)*

Before we could continue talking about sweets, Rick made a startling discovery. Three Aquatic Apes that were at my door had, in fact, followed us and were now on the path heading to the Tree of Danger.

"Quick, everyone…put on your glasses!" I could tell by the comments, subtle swears, and gasps that everyone now saw the true faces of these horrible creatures looking to destroy us. Gone were the cute, almost hypnotic stares and soft skin of these Blueies, and, in their place, thanks to the X-Ray Specs, were their true faces…glowing yellow eyes, toothy mean snarls, and skin that was almost see-through with a glowing red glob of something floating inside it. As each of my friends caught an eyeful, they began to see the situation like I did… all serious! "Don't they look like an army of Slim Goodbody's?" Again, I really thought they did.

Then I noticed something out of the corner of my eye that really worried me.

I looked down toward the moving river and I could see about ten more Aquatic Apes coming up out of the waters below us. Since we knew these woods better than anyone or anything, running from them always seemed easy before. Now they had us trapped and we had nothing to fight back with but rocks, sticks, and anything else we could find near our hole. They were on *our* turf, but we had the home field advantage. As the three on land came up to the tree, one of them was looking away and conked his dumb stupid face on the hanging branch. As he began to stumble backwards, he fell into the other two that were standing directly behind him, knocking them over. Apparently, they were very clumsy out of water. We called that a Three Stooges Move when you used the body of one to trip up another one. He let out a high-pitched, bubbly yell as he fell, which seemed like a swear word in his natural Aqua-Ape bubble language. With the commotion happening at the tree, the ones coming out of the water were distracted, looking to see what happened to their blue brothers. In the cover of nighttime and the glow of the beautiful moon, we escaped.

As we made our way back to the street, we played it off as cool as we possibly could, and, for a bunch of ten-year-old boys, I'm sure it wasn't cool at all. I wasn't sure what the Aquatic Apes had as far as technology other than those glowy balls they throw and the ability to identify people and places by their scent. At the same time, I began to understand that my friends like Missy and Edgar were becoming friendly with the Blueies, not with bad intentions, but it's because that is what us kids did…we made friends. I knew I needed to be a lot more careful than I had been in public just in case they identified me. We got to the jungle gym in the park near the pool, said our goodbyes, and planned to get together early the next morning to bring the fight to them. Of course, our meeting needed to be in a secret place, so we decided the place by the pond where we put on our skates during the winter, the place where the big kids would smoke. Everyone knew where we meant, and it was agreed we would gather everyone we could and plan what to do. But of course…not too early. Despite the excitement and chance of death, it was still summer vacation and we needed to sleep in a bit.

Apparently, Aquatic Apes didn't quite master the door handle, because, as I approached my house, there were a few of them trying to turn the knob with their big dumb webbed hands and making no progress. Wanting to avoid any unnecessary trouble, I slowly made my way to my back porch and slid the glass door open ever so quietly. As I stealthily walked into the kitchen to grab a quick snack, I saw a note pinned to the refrigerator door by one of the many FREAKIES cereal magnets that covered it.

"Who the heck was in my house while I was gone?!" I thought to myself. I was afraid to open it in the house, so I decided I just needed to leave.

I grabbed my green sleeping bag, my STAR WARS pillow, a flashlight, a couple of comic books, and made my way out to the woods…this time, deep, *deep,* DEEP in the woods…to the trestle bridge. Very rarely did we ever go to the trestle in the day, and never at night. Never…until now.

It was a long walk to the bridge that was about twenty feet above the Scantic River. Playing here could be dangerous, not to mention very far if something ever happened. Just below the bridge on the far side there was an odd little house, like a cabin, at the bottom of the hill. When Rik, Rob, Ray, and I used to play this far out we would always be tempted to go in there and see what was going on, but we were afraid to find someone living there catching us peeping in their windows. This was not a time to think. It was a time to act, and a time to survive!

It was a dark and scary walk! Despite the moon and a bright, starry night, the tree covering made light impossible to illuminate my path. I followed the train tracks very carefully to the little cabin, slid down the hill, slipped under the barbed wire fence, and quietly, like a soldier, slinked up to the front door. I looked in the front window, flashed the flashlight and saw nothing going on in there, so I decided to go on in. I opened the front door slowly and walked inside. I put all my belongings in the corner and shut the door, bracing it with a chair that was just lying there. Being a 'neat freak', I had to set up my sleeping station and organize everything. Before I settled in, I opened the note and read it by flashlight.

Dear Matt! I write what may be my final correspondence to you. First of all, I'm incredibly proud of you. You are resourceful, brave, and everything I hoped you would be when I first reached out to you. All the war comics you read and all the time you spend out in the woods playing war has prepared you for this moment.

See, I knew all that time playing in the woods would pay off…

The X-Ray Specs you found will be the most valuable piece of equipment in your battle gear. Not only do they show you the true faces of the Aquatic Apes, but they show you their one weakness. Poking or destroying their heart is the only way you can kill them. The anatomy of the Aquatic Apes is different than anything you have ever seen. As you may have already noticed their hearts move around their bodies. They were created by a diabolical mind as an unbeatable soldier and if you can't find their heart, how can you kill them? With the glasses, you can see where you need to strike to kill the enemy. Make sure when the battle is over you collect the glasses because you really *can* see through clothes. Take care, good luck, and God Speed! -Jeff

Before I could reflect on being the chosen one, the savior of the planet Earth, I heard something in the water moving around next to the cabin. The Scantic River was fairly shallow with a steady stream of water that was always moving and never very dangerous. There was never a fear of being swept away in its current because the flow never moved that quickly. The sound of the current picked up like it would after a long rain and made even the shallow water swell. As I looked out just above the window, I could see hundreds of Aquatic Apes floating by. I saw a sea of Blueies with their dumb crown-looking things just passing me by. I could hear them speaking to each other, but it wasn't in English. They sounded like hockey players, and some were even missing teeth. *"French?"* I deduced. "They're calling in troops from Montreal?"

I did all I could do and that was to wait. I slid down against the hard, cold floor and just waited until they all passed. Waited…waited…and then I prayed because I was scared and real sad.

MS. PAC-MAN
MIDWAY
Bally
MS PAC
THE BEST IN COMICS
G.I. COMBAT
GREEN LANTERN GREEN ARROW
MARVEL COMICS GROUP
INVADERS
JONAH HEX
MARVEL COMICS GROUP
CAPTAIN AMERICA
MARVEL COMICS GROUP
MICRONAUTS
MARVEL COMICS GROUP
STAR WARS
FLASH
UNKNOWN
UNEXPECTED

CHAPTER SEVEN
"It's A Miracle"

I woke up in the morning with the warm summer sun on my face. At first I was a little disoriented, waking up in a different place other than my own room, but as I woke I remembered what was going on and what was going happen. I looked out the window to see if the coast was clear and noticed the river's water level was back down again. I wrapped up my sleeping bag and left it in the corner just in case I needed to come back.

Instead of taking the more familiar way home by walking the train tracks, I decided to follow the river to our meeting place. In the time I had played down there I had never taken this path, and to be honest, I wasn't sure where it was even going to lead. I knew that eventually I would get to the pond where my crew would be waiting... or so I hoped.

About five minutes into my walk, I could hear something coming from up around the bend. Realizing I was walking right out into the open, I decided to walk off the path into the woods. Up ahead in the field were hundreds of Aquatic Apes setting up camp. There were small groups of them marching, some standing at attention, and others doing exercises. There were a few sitting around a fire which included the oddest one…a Blueie playing a harmonica, like a scene out of the American Revolution. I knew I had to get to my meeting, but I really didn't know what to do about this, or what I *could* do! I was scared. When I thought about leading people to fight these things, I never pictured their numbers being this high, or actually having to fight.

"Get it together," I told myself over and over. "People are waiting for you!" I took a deep breath, picked myself up, and climbed up a small hill to get back on track. Before I did, I had to stop at home, grab a quick snack, and brush my teeth. Despite the end of the world possibly happening, I still had an orthodontist appointment next week and needed my metal to shine.

Mill Pond Village was quiet…a little too quiet! In a building complex with over 200 units there were always a few people outside. There should be someone emptying trash, people in their cars, families out for a walk…but today, nothing. On a typical morning you would hear a symphony of car doors slamming and music playing. I walked across the playground by the pool and still…*no one*. You couldn't hear any music or TVs and that made the creepy feel, well…creepier. Then I had a thought, a really bad one. "Did the Aquatic Apes take everyone away and now I'm all alone?" As I came around the corner, I could see the woods and my path, and I just ran for it. I ran as fast as I could into the opening near the dumpster but as I started to run down the path to our meeting point, I was met by a wall of people!

"Matt, hey, Matt," Jon yelled, dressed in his favorite Seattle Seahawks t-shirt.

"Look at all the people!" I was absolutely speechless. This was half the population of the town, all gathered in the clearing in the woods, and somehow, they all fit. Everyone there had something to fight with: hockey sticks, baseball bats, bows, arrows, and even a few guns...real and BB. I knew when it all went down, I was going to be with the guys with the guns.

I walked toward the edge where the pond water met the shore and left a little trail of green slime. I looked at the other side into the willows and cattails where the Aquatic Apes were gathering. Just about a mile away the Blueies were probably getting ready for what we were preparing for…a fight to the death.

I turned around and noticed how all these people of all different backgrounds unified for one goal, our survival. Over to my right were several martial arts groups standing together as one. If there was any animosity between the different comic book ad training course groups, they were mature enough to put aside their differences for this pivotal moment, but I knew this truce would probably be short-lived. I walked in between the groups, climbed up on a big green rock to give me some height, and spoke to them.

"I'm very proud of you all," I told them, as I looked at the Black Dragon Fighting Society wearing their cool and somewhat intimidating black gees. "I know that the disciples of the late Count Dante are skilled in the arts and use the World's Deadliest Fighting Secrets so…" I looked towards the other groups, "…they will go in first." I then bowed to them, showing my respect.

"World's deadliest fighting secrets?" yelled a member of a rival faction who learned karate by record album! "How good could they be if their master, Count Dante, got in trouble for attempting to burn down a rival dojo in Chicago?! We should go in first! We are the best trained!" His group, dressed in white gees with a dynamite patch on their shoulder, roared in agreement.

OH BOY! I was hoping no one would bring up the legendary Chicago Dojo Wars of 1970. This crazy event happened when members of the Black Dragon Fighting Society stormed the Black Cobra Hall. This dojo belonged to members of the Green Dragon Society resulting in death and a lot of busted -up furniture and Count Dante in jail. Now I was losing control of the groups. I was praying no one would break into the song KUNG FU FIGHTING and start wailing on each other, but chances were good.

"Wait," said a very slender teenager, jumping in front of the groups ready to come to blows. "Sure, we have all learned from different masters and techniques found in comic book ads, but I think we can all agree on one thing…" then came the dramatic pause for effect. "No matter how we all may feel about each other, our enemy is out there, the Aquatic Apes! I represent and was trained under the International Self Defense group founded by nationally known John Natividad. He taught us to protect ourselves and our loved ones and NOT to be tatistics. I certainly don't want to be a statistic." Nice speech, Slim, but if I was going to hitch my freedom cart to anyone it was the crazies from the Black Dragon Fighting Society. They were nuts!

Then as fast as it started, the arguing got louder, mostly because the parents of the martial artists began to yell at each other. Then everything fell apart. Parents were yelling at kids, kids were yelling at other kids, and it continued to spiral out of control. I stepped off my rock and thought that even in the face of extinction, we couldn't get along. Then...something happened. We could see a figure paddling closer in a blue and white rubber raft. Man, did we all think this was the coolest thing because none of had boats or the courage to boat in the pond. As the stranger paddled toward us, people stopped fighting and began to watch this guy come closer and closer. Reaching the shallows, he jumped out of the raft and pulled it ashore. He walked into the crowd, and they began to part like the Red Sea. "Moses," I thought, and everyone began to circle around him. He looked over the gathering, caught my eye, and gave me a wink. I thought that was a bit creepy, but before I could think too much about it, he began to speak.

"We can't run into a viper's nest if we are not a unified front," the stranger said with a slight southern accent. "For some reason, these Aquatic Apes are well trained, have weapons we have no defense for, and outnumber us, but we have something they don't have!" He paused and smiled at the crowd waiting for an answer to be yelled out.

"Guns!" a guy in the back yelled out!

"The fighting skills of the Black Dragon Fighting Society" yelled another!

Obviously not getting the reply he expected, the stranger reached into his saddle bag and slowly…for dramatic effect… pulled out…in slow motion…the symbol of freedom. It was…a *Magic 8 Ball?* With the revelation of this toy, the people all stood in stunned silence. Those not in stunned silence swore a lot.

"Are we gonna throw them at the Aquatic Apes?" asked Denise, a young girl who lived on Depot Street. "I threw mine at my sister before and it gave her a black eye, so it does work."

"No, young lady," the man said, patting her on the head, "We are going to use its vast knowledge and the purplish liquid within it to plan our attacks. "If we ask the Magic 8 Ball if we should attack that Aquatic Ape patrol and the reply is SIGNS POINT TO YES then we will *attack!* If the reply is OUTLOOK NOT SO GOOD, then we will withdraw to a shelter."

This was officially the dumbest things I had ever heard, and this guy was *serious.* We were ready to be wiped out and he was talking about the Magic 8 Ball like it was real.

"We're going to trust a stupid child's toy with our lives?" a concerned and fired-up George asked, "A #$@#$ toy?!"

"A few years ago, I would have agreed with you," the mysterious man said, caressing the black orb, "but since then I have discovered all these toys in comic book ads: Aquatic Apes, X-Ray Spectacles, Silly Putty, even toy soldier sets are not what they appear to be. We live in a new age, my friends, a new world that needs us to fight for it."

He reached back into his bag, pulled out a stack of papers, and then took a moment to organize the gathered crowd into small groups. "I need twenty of you to gather all the supplies on these lists, or at least everything that you can get your hands on. Some are simple household items while others may be a little harder to come by. Gather what you can, and we shall all meet at 7 PM in the Mill across from the Opera House."

"But we can't all go in together," I told him. "If they see a ton of people going into one place then we would be trapped and taken out with one fell swoop." He smiled and winked at me again. Boy, I wish he would seriously stop doing that.

"Don't worry, Matthew," he said to me, handing out the last of his papers AND holy cow, he knows my name! "Every group has instructions on how to get there, using various entrance routes and slight variations in their times, so there will be no mass exodus arriving to raise suspicion."

"So...what do *I* do?" I asked the stranger. He began to walk away, motioning me to follow. Now I have watched a lot of TV shows where kids get kidnapped, especially in the woods never to be seen again, or become like Patty Hearst and that was not what I wanted for *me*. The stranger shook the Magic 8 Ball and read the answer to me; CANNOT PREDICT NOW. The answer made sense, so I went with him, deeper into the woods.

As we walked, I realized something…this guy was Jeff! This was the guy who has been leaving me notes, the writer of the story that started this whole crazy adventure and quite possibly the most important man alive. I was still a little worried about going in the woods with a stranger, but this wasn't a time for fear. Rather, it was a time for planning. We came to a small clearing where there was a tent pitched, a small smoldering fire, and a pot of coffee warming inside of it. As we got closer to the tent, I saw it was filled with lots of papers, books, maps, and pictures. With all this covering every inch of the area, I could see that he had a plan to not only fight these invading Aquatic Apes, but to destroy them. We made our way into the tent and Jeff motioned for me to sit.

"We have finally figured out something about these Aquatic Apes" he told me. "I have figured out why they are appearing in some towns and not others, and, with that information, I have deduced how to destroy them." I was intrigued. "Broad Brook, New Haven, parts of Enfield, Norwalk, New Britain, just to name a few. This is where the Aquatic Apes outbreaks first began. Why these towns and not others? The common denominator is the water in these towns has fluoride in it! Something about the physical makeup of the Aquatic Ape mixed with fluorinated water has created the monstrosity we see before us. Even Montreal, Canada, has fluorinated water!"

This made complete sense to me…well, sort of. I mean it made sense that something was creating these freaky things, but I didn't know how fluoride became the magic ingredient. All I knew about fluoride was that it strengthened your teeth and kept the Cavity Creeps away. And what caused cavities? "Oh my God," I yelled feeling like I just discovered the meaning of life, *"Sugar!"*

"Ahhhh, very good, grasshopper," Jeff said as he rolled out a big map on the table. "We aren't going to be fighting Aquatic Apes with conventional weapons. We are going to use white gold…" he reached his hand into a big bag of sugar and sifted a handful through his fingers, letting it drop back into the bag, *"Caribbean S!"*

As I sat down and got comfortable, Jeff showed me his plan for how we were going to win this war. He reached under the table and pulled out a G.I. Joe Footlocker, a green military box that you would store all your G.I. Joe gear in. The box was marked "Explosives" so of course I got pretty excited. He then reached in and took out what looked like a water balloon. At first I thought, "what the heck are we gonna do with that, hit a car and run?" Jeff placed it carefully on the table, stepped back a little, and then studied it like it was a special gold coin from the Franklin Mint. "It may look like an ordinary water balloon, but to an Aquatic Ape this is instant death." He then had a weird smile on his face. "And if it isn't instant death, it's sure going to hurt a lot."

"What's inside it?" I asked.

"It is a simple water balloon filled with soda," he said proudly. "But it has to be a sugar pop…no TAB or Fresca! It has got to be the hard stuff. Saccharine doesn't have the same effect as the pure sugar cane. Then the balloon is placed in a Ziplock sandwich bag and loaded with Pop Rocks and maple syrup."

The very idea of mixing soda and Pop Rocks had been an obsession for us kids since we first heard about the tragic death of Mikey from the Life cereal commercials. Despite any warnings, we all wanted to do it, but none of us had the courage to follow through.

"Let me explain how this weapon will work," Jeff said picking up bag. "The soda in the balloon is loaded with sugar. When the balloon hits an Aquatic Ape, it will break, sending the now shaken soda flooding into the cheap baggie, igniting the Pop Rocks. The maple syrup will cause the soda and exploding Pop Rocks to stick to its target, slowly eating away its blue skin until it springs a leak and dies."

"Death by Pop Rocks," I thought… just like Mikey! "Will it work?" I asked.

"It better," he said as he walked over to a hanging map of Broad Brook. "If not, then this will be one short rebellion! The battle plan calls for the fights to be taken to the streets, broken down to several different areas. We will have the battle start before the bridge, slowly move between the Mill and the Opera House, and culminate at the Fire Station." Jeff then got in a seriously tough guy pose and gave a speech that shook the foundation. "We shall fight them at the reservoir, we shall fight them on the playgrounds, we shall fight them in the tobacco fields, and in the streets, we shall in Prospect Hills, we shall never surrender!"

Hmmmmm, not bad.

Jeff just stood there for a moment, probably listening to his words echo around his brain and then hearing the applause generating in his own head. After about ten minutes, he finally snapped back to reality and handed me a piece of paper. On it was my part in the plan, nicely typed and very official looking.

5 PM - Meet the rest of your team on the Main Street Bridge, Mill side. Set up 6 on each side. The rest will hide behind garbage can barricades in front of the bridge.

5:15 PM – Start a commotion that will draw the Aquatic Ape army to you. When they are close enough, ask the Magic 8 Ball if you should attack. If Yes, you will attack. If No, you will retreat to the fire station and assist the other teams in their assault.

8:00 PM - If we win, that is good, and it'll be a good night! If not, then you and the survivors head to the free zones of Massachusetts.

"What is the rest of the plan?" I asked him, knowing I was only getting a small piece of it.

"I can't tell you the rest, for security reasons," Jeff told me. "I'm the only one who knows the full plan, but if everyone does their part then we will be waking up tomorrow victorious." Jeff began to walk out of the tent, "Victorious and *Free!* If not...."

Okay, this was it. There was no turning back now.

At the Sign of THE UNHOLY THREE

Are you willing to PUT IN PAWN to the UNHOLY THREE all of the material, mental and spiritual resources of this GREAT REPUBLIC?

FLUORIDATED WATER

1—Water containing Fluorine (rat poison—no antidote) is already the only water in many of our army camps, making it very easy for saboteurs to wipe out an entire camp personel. If this happens, every citizen will be at the mercy of the enemy—already within our gates.

POLIO SERUM

2—Polio Serum, it is reported, has already killed and maimed children; its future effect on minds and bodies cannot be guaged. This vaccine drive is the entering wedge for nation-wide socialized medicine, by the U. S. Public Health Service, (heavily infiltrated by Russian-born doctors, according to Congressman Clare Hoffman.) In enemy hands it can destroy a whole generation.

MENTAL HYGIENE

3—Mental Hygiene is a subtle and diabolical plan of the enemy to transform a free and intelligent people into a cringing horde of zombies.

Rabbi Spitz in the American Hebrew, March 1, 1946: "American Jews must come to grips with our contemporary anti-Semites; we must fiil our insane asylums with anti-Semitic lunatics."

FIGHT COMMUNISTIC WORLD GOVERNMENT by destroying THE UNHOLY THREE ! ! !   It is later than you think!

KEEP AMERICA COMMITTEE
H. W. Courtois, Secy.

Box 3094, Los Angeles 54, Calif.

May 16, 1955

Brook, CT

CHAPTER EIGHT
"Daybreak"

It was 4:45 PM, fifteen minutes until zero hour! For mood music, I put on K-Tel's "Hit Machine" on 8-Track! "Twenty original hits...Twenty original stars including... "I spoke in my best TV announcer voice, "KC and the Sunshine Band… Elton John…Maxine Nightingale…John Sebastian! Double-album only $5.99, tape only $7.99!" The music would set the tone and help me get myself ready for whatever was about to happen.

I went into my closet and found clothes that said this guy was ready for war! I put on my camouflage pants, mud-stained white Converse sneakers, and my favorite KISS shirt, featuring the band in their Spirit of '76 pose. I cut off the sleeves for better mobility, and, of course, to show off my muscles. I threw on a New York Cosmos wristband and then went into my sister's room for a little bit of makeup to cover my face. Since she took most of her stuff when she left with my parents, I had to work with what she had...that green stuff she put on at night went all over my face. Black eyeliner went under my eyes and some Good & Plenty-flavored Bonnie Bell Lip Smackers to keep my lips moist and hydrated because…well, just because. Please don't judge me.

And now I was ready!

As I walked down the path to my rendezvous with destiny, I began to wonder if this was the last time I would walk on this very trail. Reflectively I studied every single leaf and rock and noticed how cool the bright, setting sun looked as it set through the trees and shone off the slime of the shimmering pond. How many times did I walk this exact way and not notice the beauty and serenity? Well, I'm a ten-year-old, so I don't notice those things.

I got to the bridge to meet with my team who were there waiting for me. Matthew and his brother William were already in a fight about what to call our group, because that's what kids do. Matthew wanted "The Batmen" and his brother wanted us to be called "Team Crusade." Both names were completely out of the question, and we really didn't have time to discuss it any further. To stop them from fighting I put them in charge of some of our special weapons, LITTLE HUGS, the all-sugar fruit juice barrel drink! We brought them as an easy grenade-type-throwing-weapon in case they were needed. Simply use your front teeth to puncture the foil top and throw. Unfortunately, Matthew and William were drinking them instead of getting them ready for action. 5 PM was only a few minutes away and we had to create a diversion to draw the Aquatic Apes away from their base of operations at the carnival grounds.

"OK, it's time," I declared, nervous, getting ready to execute the diversion. "So, who has the Magic 8 Ball?" Stephen, who normally didn't hang out with us because he went to Catholic School, raised his hand holding the mystical black orb. I took it from him very carefully, looked at the big black 8, and asked, "Is it time?" I turned the ball over slowly, waiting for the answer to appear. WITHOUT A DOUBT it told me, so I handed it back to Stephen and addressed the troops.

   "This is what we're gonna do. Jon and I are going to run up the street as far as we can and try to get the Aquatic Apes to chase us. We will wait for them on the bridge, and, when they are in eyeshot, we're gonna pelt them with balloons." As we got ready to go, the group moved four large garbage cans out into the middle of the street. Inside each can was a large supply of water balloon grenades ready for the throwing. On both sides of the bridge, the rest of the team was getting out their homemade bombs, lining them up on the street or the bridge railing, ready for action. Jon and I started up the street and every once-in-a-while would take a look back to see everyone watching us as we neared our date with destiny. I just thought of that phrase now. Back then I was just thinking about not 'making' in my pants. Well, it's the truth.

   To keep our minds off what we were about to do, and what might happen to us, Jon and I had nervous conversations, mostly about football. "Wouldn't it be cool if someday our favorite teams played each other in the Super Bowl?" Jon asked. "When donkeys fly" I replied, doing my best Flo impersonation from the TV show, ALICE. It was such a longshot anyway, considering my beloved New England Patriots and his Seattle Seahawks weren't very good, and probably never would be, but we needed to focus on something positive, no matter how long a shot it was. After all, we were going to make big Aquatic Apes chase us… so how much crazier could *that* be?

   "Aquatic Apes….Come out to plaaayyy-eeeyaaaayyyyy!" Jon whispered, clanking a couple of dirty soda bottles together. Okay, this made me relax a bit. The Warriors was a great movie.

   Walking up the street, we could see a collection of Blueies in the soccer fields at the Middle School, so we thought we would start there. As we entered the schoolyard, Jon and I realized this was where we needed to reveal ourselves and try to get as many of them as we could to chase us. The problem was that there were a lot of them, all just waiting. Our nerves were starting to become stronger than rational thought and out of nowhere, like Damien in THE OMEN movie, Jon became like a boy possessed! He ran out onto the field and certainly let them know we were there!

   "Hey, you stupid @#$%^ blue, dumb @#$%^, #$%^&* pieces of @#$%^& who do nothing but @#$%%^ to your stupid @#$%^&*!"

   First of all, I was a little shocked at the words that were coming out of his mouth. Sure, I knew most of those words from watching SATURDAY NIGHT FEVER, but I never heard them used in such a way. If my mother ever heard Jon talk like that, she would never let me hang out with him again. If *his* mother ever heard those words…well, I may never see Jon again. Second, he just ran by me screaming as a group of about a hundred Blueies began to run to where we were, so I bolted like the Six Million Dollar Man down the street yelling to alert everyone.

"The Aquatic Apes are coming, the Aquatic Apes are coming!"

Running back to our position on the bridge, I could see the group getting ready to begin their assault of balloon fury. I don't know how many were behind me and I was afraid to look. I didn't know where Jon went off to. I knew he wasn't *with* me. Did he get *captured*...or *worse?* I knew he didn't get lost, because the town is so small and every street and backyard connected with every other one. Then, without warning, something hit me in the face and it hit me real hard! It was a balloon thrown a bit low and short that was meant for an Ape. It stunned me for a second but once I realized what it was, I thought it tasted really good, especially with the Pop Rocks. As I made it back to the bridge, Robert came running up and told me he threw that one and was sorry.

"Not as sorry as we will *all* be if we don't start taking out some apes!" I yelled.

As low Main Street began to fill up with Blueies, they did something real strange. The Aquatic Apes all just stood in one spot until they slowly got into an odd formation, eleven pinkies across and five rows back. With a mental cue, they began to move, not directly at us but moving side to side and then a step forward, in unison. Wait. I knew this! I'd seen it *before!*

"They are working a classic Space Invaders attack maneuver," I yelled. "Hurry up everyone! Get behind the four garbage cans!" Some of our group was wielding shields, well… plastic garbage can lids. We did learn in science that rubber or plastic didn't conduct electricity, so the cans may be our best defense. I wasn't sure what these lids were made of but they did say Rubbermaid on them so I assumed *rubber.*

As they started to move closer to our position in a sort of hypnotic and rather menacing way, the Aquatic Apes in the back began throwing their glowing energy balls at us. We hid as best we could behind the plastic garbage cans. Then it was our turn to turn up the heat. The skies filled with water balloons arcing toward the oncoming creatures, some missing by a mile but others hitting their targets dead on! It was an incredible sight to behold when a balloon would strike its target. As the contents splashed their blue skin, you could see and hear the Pop Rocks begin to sizzle, finding their way into the creatures held in position by the maple syrup. Then, in a *flash*, the hit Aquatic Ape began to shake until their bodies sprang a leak at the point of impact. Within seconds the fluid of each would drain out and crumble to the ground, leaving a weird-smiling blue empty husk in its place. The husk would then roll away in the gentle breeze or be trampled by the Aquatic Apes behind it. We needed to see a lot of that!!!

They got closer. I turned my head to left, and saw Kenny on his E.I. Walkie Talkie with Morse Code Transmitter and Code Key. Like Kenny, a few of us cut out coupons and sent in $12.95 plus $2.00 postage and insurance for one of those, and now they were helping to ensure our victory. In the heat of battle, I saw Kenny sending Morse-Coded messages to his friend Christopher, who had picked a really bad time to visit him from Ohio.

As the Blueies were attacking and overwhelming us, I could hear Kenny sending his coded messages to Chris. BEEP-BEEP-BEEEEP-BEEP-BEEP! I could see Chris following the key to see what Kenny was saying. BEEP-BEEEEEEEP-BEEP-BEEP-BEEEEEEEEP! The more they coded to each other, the closer we came to being overrun by the Blueies. I yelled to Kenny to just tell Chris what the message was, since he was literally four feet away from him, though I did understand wanting to use the Morse Code feature because it was so much cooler.

As the Aquatic Apes got closer to us, but less in numbers, they began moving faster and faster toward our position.

"Keep throwing," I yelled, not seeing the new group of Blueies marching in the same formation just a bit behind that group. "We have got to hold this bridge!" I could see that in both Kenny and Christopher's eyes as they looked to their right side with panic! To the right of us, coming out of the pond, we could see about 50 or 60 more Aquatic Apes rising from the green slime and coming up on shore. As they got closer, we saw that their blue skin covered in the green slime made them slippery and thus impervious to the sticky bombs we were chucking at them. We shifted our defenses and began to chuck at them in full force. Then I realized something as I saw their berets! "OH NO!!! Singes aquatiques à notre droite," I yelled, motioning for the group to pull back, "French Aquatic Apes to our right!" As our defenses became overwhelmed, I made a decision I didn't want to make. "Pull back to the fire house! Everyone *fall back*!" I felt like such a failure because I couldn't do my job. I couldn't hold the bridge.

Everyone started screaming, retreating, and returning fire in between. If this was our Alamo, we would go down fighting…or running. Running was good, too. I looked at our crew dodging energy balls and noticed that Vaughn was missing.

"Where's Vaughn?!" I yelled, panicking that we may have lost another soldier. Out of breath, Dave told me that he had to go the bathroom really bad so he went into Pigeons to pee. That sounded about right for Vaughn. He would get a hit playing baseball and stand on first screaming, "I gotta pee!" Good old Vaughn. He wasn't old. He was 10. But I really like that phrase.

I thought things couldn't get any worse…but they did. Our friend Stephanie was put in charge of supplies because she was by far way more responsible than the rest of us. Responsible for the balloon bomb distribution, she came running up to tell me news that I knew was going to be bad. "Matt, we're running out of balloon bombs." So we moved back between the Mill and Opera House. She shouted to the troops, "We need to pull back *faster* because phase two is going to happen soon!"

Phase *Two?* What was this Phase Two Stephanie spoke of?

As we made our way to the next position, I saw movement on the rooftops of the Opera House and the Mill. In the windows of the two buildings, I saw people with rifles, bows, and a few slingshots ready to fire as Aquatic Apes passed by. It was such a relief to see people ready to help us out and all wearing X-Ray Specs. "Fire at the floating red thing inside their bodies," someone yelled!

"That's the only way to take 'em down!" I yelled. Then what happened next was a spectacle to see and hear. Like the 4th of July, you could hear the non-stop pop bangs, and ka-blamms echoing up the street. When the first volley ended and the smoke cleared, the street was filled with dead Aquatic Apes. But there were still more living ones, who were now as angry as a broken hornet's nest. I looked at Stephanie who had that "this is not going well" look on her face.

Surviving Aquatic Apes started to break their video game formation and proceeded to hustle into the Mill to bring the battle inside its dark and echo-filled halls. I could see flashes of light in the empty windows and cracks in the walls. The Blueies and I knew they we were losing the battle inside. Soon after, from within, there came the screaming of humans being taken down. Out back of the derelict building, people were funneling from every opening, running to join us in our retreat.

"We did all we could," said Bryan, holding his leg which was burned by an energy ball and looked kinda gross. "We lost some of people but so did they!" I didn't know what to say to him, but there was really no need, because we both knew we did our job as best we could.

"We can't stop this now," Nicholas said to us, trying to be reassuring! "It's like being a catcher...you call the game, make sure everyone is where they need to be, and always wear your cup!" Usually he just talks about soccer, but right now we needed Gary Carter, Carlton Fisk and a 'cup'.

We made our way between the fire trucks parked out in the middle of Main Street placed there for defensive purposes. Me and a few others made it into the fire station, an old brick building that, despite its run-down look, served this town well. I was hoping that this building was not going to be where we made our last stand. The last time I walked into this building I was given a plastic fire hat with a rubber band strap and a TOT FINDER sticker that I proudly put on my bedroom window. We all gathered into the open space of the building now that all the fire trucks were parked at the bottom of the driveway.

With the fire trucks blocking Main Street, its hoses at the ready, we had a not-bad blockade. Although I thought that the pressure of the water could probably knock the Blueies down, I didn't think using fire trucks was a great plan. In charge of the Main Street defense were Alan and Chris, two brothers from Boston who were working with our volunteer firefighters. Alan brought with him an expertise on using an ax and getting into his boots quickly. Chris not only brought with him his accent, but his ability to save kittens stranded in tall trees while looking good doing it! The Hebert brothers picked a bad time to come to our little town, but for us, they were right where they needed to be.

The firehouse was full with what appeared to be the entire surviving population of Broad Brook. With that there was a lot of noise and chaos as well as a huge line for the bathroom. Out back, I could see various groups planning their next parts of the attack, but all was not fun and games. I saw Keith, Amy, and John from the Leominster Guardians who were in charge of defending the sewage treatment plant at the end of Mill Street. It was a tough detail because the thought was that the Aquatic Apes originated from the place we call the Filter Beds. Sadly the Leominster Guardians lost most of its group.

"There was dissension within the ranks," Amy told me while trying to catch her breath," but we three had the vision to carry on." With her words, Keith perked up and looked at John, who was standing there for some reason without a shirt.

"How good?" Keith yelled to his friend.

"So Good!" John replied, checking his reflection in the window. These guys were a little crazy, but loyal and always looking to help. We needed a little crazy!

Joining The Leominster Guardians was a small group from New Jersey who called themselves the Jersey Devils, a super-cool name. I didn't even know where New Jersey was, but I was so thankful that Jackson, Ariana, and Joseph's family deciding to visit friends on Old Ellington Road, jumping into action when they smelled the commotion. Yeah, sometimes commotions have a smell.

"We saw some escape behind the gas station," Jackson said, running right toward the enemy without a thought for his own safety.

"Those things are not going to escape!" Ariana said, running behind Jackson with Joseph right behind him. Jackson was the quiet one of the group, but I wouldn't want to have to fight him, or any of them, because they were *tough, Jersey Tough!* I was glad that they were on our side.

In the corner by the brick fire pit, I found Stephen who looked as scared like the rest of us. When I walked up to him, I took the Magic 8 Ball from his hands and asked it the question I wasn't sure I wanted an answer to. "Will we *survive* this?" I turned it over slowly to reveal the answer, REPLY HAZY, TRY AGAIN! Uh oh…not good! I dropped it and ran.

Knowing that Aquatic Apes were heading up the street towards our position, I made my way through the building past babies crying, people yelling, and overall confusion. People were hurting, both physically and emotionally, and many understandably had just given up, but I wasn't about to roll over and live under the blue webbed feet of tyranny. I was going to fight, and, if be, die trying to be free. I didn't want to die, but well, y'know, whatever.

In one of the bigger offices, I could see people making more sugar balloon bombs with everything and anything they could find. If they couldn't find sugar soda, they just filled water balloons with milk and Sweet & Low packets. Whatev would work to slow the Aquatic Apes down. The survivors of the Mill were taking position on the roof of the fire station as well as the small package store in front of it. Rifles and bows were poised to fire, all wearing X-Ray Specs and ready to do whatever was necessary to win this fight.

"They're coming up from behind us!" someone yelled as a few people went to the hill side of the building to do what they could to fight off this new attack fror the rear.

"Those Blueies are looking to Malachi Crunch us," I yelled, watching as another group of Aquatic Apes moved toward us from the other side of Main Street, attempting to overrun us. I kept looking around for Jeff to help us, to put togeth a plan to save us all at the last minute, until I realized our destiny was in our own hands and we only had ourselves to rely on.

I thought about how, a few years ago, we celebrated the American Bicentennia It was then that I really began to study and enjoy learning about the battles of th American Revolution, our first fight for freedom. As a lover of history, I was a big fan of these events and tales of heroism in the face of adversity like Bunker Hill or where it was really fought, Breed's Hill. What I wasn't a very big fan of was how that story ended…with a lot of death and an American loss.

As I positioned myself outside next to one of the fire trucks, a water tanker, I could see the group we were fighting earlier a little thinner in numbers but still moving toward us. Reaching into a garbage can for a water balloon bomb, I found something hard at the bottom. I pulled it out and saw that it was another Magic 8 Ball. Knowing I shouldn't ask it I did anyway. "Magic 8 Ball, will we survive this?" I turned it over carefully and cautiously, hoping to force a better reply than I did last time…DON'T COUNT ON IT, it said. "Uh-oh!"

Across the street, a group of people were hiding on the side of the bank, throwing water balloons and small lollipops. Despite being the only bank in tow I was always disappointed that they only had small, one-bite suckers, but there they were, now being thrown at the invaders and doing a little harm. The pop would stick and seem to annoy them until they pulled it off. Then it would eat through their skin, causing them to leak. Seeing this I grew a bit optimistic. Here, ordinary, everyday people were fighting because their lives depended on it. I saw Mrs. Johnson, the old, short bank attendant throwing balloons with considerable accuracy and taking out three Aquatic Apes with as many throws. "Joker, Joker, Joker!" she yelled, watching the now-empty husks fall on the steps of the bank.

Wow, maybe we had a chance!

Showing no respect for our One God System, the Aquatic Apes began to storm the steps of the Congregational Church where parishioners were there waiting with bags of sugar, just chucking handfuls of the white stuff right in the faces of the attackers, blinding them and eventually taking the fight right out of them. It seemed that any advantage we may have had was met with just more Aquatic Apes. Now, there were Blueies traveling up Mill Street towards our fire truck barricade that didn't seem to do anything other than make them walk around it, but we just kept on fighting. Energy balls were exploding all around us and I knew they were hitting people because I could hear screaming and swearing coming from every direction. Confusion seemed to become stronger among us with every explosion, but still we fought on.

As their circle of death began to tighten around us, we were thinking that the end, our end, was near. There were so many people hiding in the fire station that were depending on us to keep them alive, but we were failing, and we needed a miracle. As we huddled around the trucks, Fire Chief Brian LeTendre began to move toward one of the hoses. As he got to the front of it and struggled to pull it up, I saw George, a wannabe fireman climb up on the truck and begin to push buttons, spin wheels, and yell to the chief, "Get ready, boss! The pressure is building slow but steady," and gave him the much-coveted thumbs up! Now I have seen enough cartoons and movies like the TOWERING INFERNO to know that you need more than one person to hold the hose or you'll just get whipped around like…well, something crazy being whipped around. So, I left my position, got behind Chief LeTendre, and grabbed the hose. This thing was heavy, and we needed more than an old man and a little kid to do this. Suddenly, out of every hiding space, people came out to help us. Everyone grabbed a section of hose and held on for dear life.

From my angle I couldn't see it, but I knew this act was being repeated on the other fire truck behind us. People from all walks of life, an executive at LEGO, a tobacco picker, and a deli guy at Chester's were all coming together. No matter your economic situation or how you dressed, today we were one, manning hoses and getting ready for the big explosion of water to fly. I did realize that the pressured water flying out of the hoses would only knock them back, maybe disorient them for a few precious seconds, and give those in hiding a chance to run and hide, but what happened next was nothing short of the miracle that I, and probably many others, were praying for.

"Hold on, everyone," yelled the Chief, "Here comes a little party favor for our uninvited guests!" What came jetting out of the hose wasn't exactly the water we expected. It was a thick, red, fluffy substance that, when it left the hose, a little spray came back to hit us. It was sticky and sweet, and I licked my lips to get a flavor. *"Cherry,"* I thought to myself? Then I would get my answer from the Chief. "Thanks to the boys at the Enfield Fire Department and complements from the 7-Eleven on Weymouth Road…Slurpees!" *Slurpees?* Oh, man, this stuff was nothing but liquid sugar! I would have thought of this if we had a 7-Eleven in our town, but we didn't.

The Slurpees were a perfect weapon against these things, because they must be the unhealthiest, yet most delicious treat on the entire planet. There was nothing healthy and redeeming in a Slurpee, but man I would pound those things down, especially when they would be in a cool Marvel Comics superhero cup. Today, in Broad Brook, Cherry Slurpees were saving lives. Like our homemade balloon bombs but fast acting, this delicious spray was loaded with sugar and all kinds of sticky. The Slurpee hoses were working just as well on the other side of us, but in a different delicious flavor, Coca-Cola!

For us, it was an amazing sight to see! First the Aquatic Apes would get knocked back about ten feet from the concussion and usually knock over a few more on the way down. Then, they would be covered in this sticky solution that would begin to eat right through them. Their numbers were beginning to thin down on all sides, but we still weren't out of the woods yet.

Joining the fight was Dairy Mart owner Romano and his wife, Kelly, who had their own small army of customers with their own weapons. Coming in from the top of the hill was Team Slush Puppy, who were attacking by throwing full cups of Slush Puppies. Cherry, strawberry, orange and blue raspberry treats were hurled at the blueies, and, while not as fast-acting as the Slurpees, still did the trick. There would be years of debate as to what was better, Slurpees or Slush Puppies. I have my opinion, but that day they were both the food of the gods!

Suddenly and without anyone even realizing it, the battle was over...and we had won. Every Aquatic Ape that was attacking us, every single one of them, was gone. Just as fast as they first arrived, they were now just empty husks all over the street. I walked to the fire truck and reached for the Magic 8 Ball, curious to ask it another question.

"Magic 8 Ball, is it really all over?" I asked, even though I felt what the answer was, because, it was the Magic 8 Ball. Who was I compared to it? SIGNS POINT TO YES! Yes.

Instead of everyone celebrating like they do in the movies, by hugging and throwing their hats into the air, everyone just looked at each other. It may have been the fact that most of us were covered in red or brown sticky syrup, or it could have had more to do with the fact that we were just exhausted and didn't quite know how to react. It could also have been a sugar crash, but it was still an emotional and trying time for all of us. For the past however long it was, we had lived in constant fear of being enslaved and or destroyed by the Aquatic Apes. We watched our friends caged like animals, we saw families disappear, never to be heard from again, and we knew that this was being repeated in other towns suffering the same fate as we had. Our hopes and prayers were about wanting their victory to be as sweet as ours. I swore I could hear "We Are The Champions" by Queen playing in the background. That day, we were the champions.

"As long as there are drinks containing real and natural sugar and delicious candies," said Reverend Peterson, the main man of the Congregational Church, "there will be victory." Everyone in earshot agreed with him and nodded, no matter what their faith. Then they gathered their family members and friends and made the long walk home.

We knew that a few Aquatic Apes probably got away and we weren't sure at the time how other towns were faring in the battle, but we knew that in the tiny town of Broad Brook, Connecticut, the people rose up, joined together, and won.

Over the next few days newspapers and TV reports would tell of something happening, but no one would mention anything about the truth of HOW and WHY it happened. There was speculation from the No Nukes people about some "toxic chemicals getting into the water systems, contaminating microscopic plankton, and creating mutated creatures." Environmentalists explained that dangerous stuff was leaking into the water supplies from town dumps. People could guess all they wanted, but we knew the truth…or at least I knew the truth!

A crazy scientist playing God created life that, when mixed with fluoridated water, would grow and grow and grow. It wasn't just the fluoride that birthed these creatures. It was an evil that had created it, an evil that has no place in this world. Sadly, this evil professor would disappear once again like he did following the end of World War Two. Although he would go into hiding, he would keep creating ways to take over the world, never coming as close as he did in the Summer of 1979.

And what about Jeff? Sadly, I would never see or hear from him again. Following the fight in Broad Brook, I heard from a very reliable source that he was involved in the victorious battle in New Haven and then made his way up North to Montreal, Quebec, Canada to take care of their Ape problem. Somehow, a little bit of Jeff will always remain in the hearts of everyone from the little town that once had a big Aquatic Ape problem.

CHAPTER NINE
"Ready To Take A Chance Again"

As the sun began to rise on a brand-new day, life seemed to be getting back to some sense of normalcy for us. It's amazing how the extinction of the human rac can come and go and feel like, after a little bit of cleaning up and a load of laundry, that it's back to business as usual. Cars began to roll back into our little building complex which was sadly about sixty units less than it was at the beginning of this story. Townhouse Road was pretty narrow, and it didn't take much for a traffic jam to happen. The Hayes family drove by waving, as did the Noel clan in their beat-up yellow and rust-colored truck. Heather and Steven waved and got my attention as their dog, named Dog (but pronounced Dio-gee) was going crazy in the cab, trying to be controlled by Mr. and Mrs. Noel. Rochelle sat in the back and waved, but that is all I got. Steven and Heather kept waving and I waved back, until the awkwardness of them sitting in the same spot for the last five minutes hit all of us.

I went back outside to see more people returning and had to catch my breath a bit, reflecting on the previous day's events, and waiting for my family to return.

Whatever happened to Jon? Following our getting chased by Aquatic Apes at the Middle School, he ran through the backyards on Church Street until he hit th Mason's yard. Jon didn't know there was a low-hanging dog chain going across the yard and clotheslined himself into unconsciousness, missing the entire battle And he had one heck of a welt across his head.

I was quite relieved when the Card family pulled up in a taxi. As they got out of the car and got their bags, they waved, and Andra and Jason came running over to see me, oblivious to what had just happened.

"How was Cincinnati?" I asked both of them. Proudly wearing their new Cincinnati Reds baseball caps, they told me how much fun they had visiting family and showed me some of the things they got. Jay pulled out some comic books and a STAR WARS poster magazine that he bought at the airport. Andra opened up her bag and pulled out a little clear case full of sand. As I looked a little closer, I could see something scurrying around inside kicking up the sand until it revealed itself.

"It's a CRAZY CRAB," Andra told me quite excited. "It's the new live sensation that's sweeping America. You can buy them in the back of comic books."

CRAZY CRAB? I saw another war on the horizon...

(NOT) THE END

BROAD BROOK
Est. 1892
OPERA HOUSE
107 Main Street
Broad Brook, CT 06018
860.558.9202
www.broadbrookoperahouse.com

    My heartfelt thanks to the musicians who supported this book with their heart and soul - their music. Without your generous gifts, this book would just be...a book! Now, it's an experience! - *Matman*

'From The Sea' performed by Alice Loves Alien
Gina Andia – lead vocal, harmony, and background vocals
Brendan Clark – lead vocal, harmony and background vocals, lead. Rhythm and acoustic guitars, organ, synth, bass, drums, hand claps, percussion
Lyrics and Music written by Brendan Clark - Mysticism and Mischief Music (BMI)
Produced and engineered by Brendan Clark, Mixed and mastered by Jim Fogarty
Recorded at Interstellar Cosmic Studios
www.alicelovesalien.com

'Hey Boy' written and performed by Amanda Meli
Production by Mark Thayer (co-founder of signature sound)
www.youtube.com/@AmandaMeli

'Aphasia' performed by Livesay
Gregg Livesay – guitars
Tony Stahl – keyboards
Alan D'Angelo - bass
Tim Huntington - drums
Written by Gregory P. Livesay – Livesaymusic (BMI)
www.livesaybandofficial.com

'Rest Of My Days' written and performed by Scott Fish
Scott Fish – vocals and acoustic guitar
Mark Mikel – bass and drums
Tony Papa - lead acoustic guitar
Produced by Mark Mikel and Scott Fish
©Copyright 1996 L. Scott Fish
www.youtube.com/@battledrumacoustica

read the book...listen to the soundtrack! AVAILABLE NOW!

Featuring the hit single **FROM THE SEA** by Alice Loves Alien
the beautiful **HEY BOY** by Amanda Meli
the intense **APHASIA** performed by Livesay
the whimsical **REST OF MY DAYS** by Scott Fish
with mood music performed by The Axolotl Orchestra

fill your **BOOM BOX**, Console, Car Stereo or HiFi system
with amazing music on sale now at these fine retailers: